JASMINE SUMMER

Verity is delighted when Jake Thornton, the new owner of March Place, offers her the contract to design The Lady Mary Thornton Garden. She loves her work but her life is beset with problems. The other members of the garden team are hostile towards her and, although she is attracted to Jake, their relationship is far from smooth. And then there is Tara Fraser-Ellis, who is determined to marry Jake and sees Verity as a rival.

JEAN M. LONG

JASMINE SUMMER

WORCESTERSHIRE COUNTY COUNCIL
CULTURAL SERVICES

Complete and Unabridged

LINFORD
Leicester

First published in Great Britain in 2004

First Linford Edition
published 2005

British Library CIP Data

Long, Jean M.
    Jasmine summer.—Large print ed.—
Linford romance library
    1. Love stories
    2. Large type books
    I. Title
    823.9'14 [F]

    ISBN 1–84395–586–5

Published by
F. A. Thorpe (Publishing)
Anstey, Leicestershire

Set by Words & Graphics Ltd.
Anstey, Leicestershire
Printed and bound in Great Britain by
T. J. International Ltd., Padstow, Cornwall

This book is printed on acid-free pape

1

It was peaceful in the grounds of March Place. Verity inhaled the fragrant air, thinking it had been an inspiration to stop off here during her lunch break. She had parked in the lane, hoping to catch a glimpse of the azaleas, but then, on finding the side gate unlocked, had slipped inside.

The azaleas were even lovelier than she had remembered from previous years, a myriad of exquisite blooms ranging from purest white through pastel shades to scarlet and fiery orange. Slowly, she made her way among them, stopping here and there to examine the delicate flowers. She was a pretty girl with a mass of honey-blonde hair and large dark-blue eyes. Her petite frame was encased in shabby denim overalls and a faded T-shirt.

Reaching the path once more, she realised she was being watched. Undaunted, she drew nearer, noting that the man was tall with lean, finely-chiselled features and a thatch of light-brown hair and that he had a camera slung around his neck. His slate-green eyes appraised her coolly for a long moment until she broke the silence.

'They're magnificent, aren't they?'

'They certainly are, very photogenic. I suppose you wouldn't care to pose for me.'

She was taken aback.

'You suppose right. Anyway, I've got to go or I'll be late.'

'A pity! You're pretty photogenic yourself, you know. Anyway, I've taken a couple of shots already.'

'You've got a nerve!' she exclaimed.

He fell into step beside her.

'Most young women would be flattered. If you'll let me have your name and address I'll send you some prints.'

Verity fixed him with an indignant stare.

'That's an original pick-up line, if ever I heard one! I'm not interested so you can just forget it.'

He looked genuinely surprised and then began to laugh.

'Oh, dear, I'm afraid you've completely misconstrued the situation. Let me explain.'

She waved his explanation aside impatiently.

'No time, and, if I were you, I'd watch out for the groundsman. He doesn't take kindly to intruders wandering about, so be warned!'

To her irritation, he totally ignored this last remark.

'Please yourself, but it's your loss. I'm told I'm a pretty good photographer!'

The cheek of the man! She hurried away, her contentment shattered. Putting him out of her mind, she concentrated on getting back to Hollybanks before Ralph got annoyed again.

She couldn't afford to fall out with her right-hand man. Ever since her parents had gone on holiday to Australia, leaving her in charge of the nursery, things had been going wrong. First her grandfather had had an accident, hurting his leg, so that he was confined to the house for the time being. Then a couple of their most reliable part-timers had left to work at the new garden centre on the other side of Oakhurst. The increased work-load had put them all under pressure and Ralph, usually so amiable, had suddenly become dis-gruntled and moody.

Verity completed her delivery round in record time and returned to Hollybanks along a series of winding lanes. The rambling Kentish, ragstone house was looking distinctly shabby these days, she thought sadly, but there was no money to spare for renovations. Every last penny was ploughed back into the business which had been going through a rocky patch recently.

Her grandfather and Mrs Jolly, their

treasured domestic help, were drinking tea at the ancient kitchen table.

'Sit down, lass,' he said, sounding so dejected that she was alarmed.

'What's wrong, Grandpa?' she asked anxiously.

'It's Ralph. He's given in his notice.'

She stared at him open-mouthed.

'But why? I thought he was happy here.'

'He's been offered promotion and more money so who can blame him for accepting?'

Light suddenly dawned.

'Don't tell me he's going to work at that new place as well?'

He sighed deeply and she took this to be a 'yes'.

'I'd have thought better of Ralph,' she said slowly. 'That place, whatever it's called, must have offered him a tidy incentive.'

'The Garden Trug', Mrs Jolly supplied the name.

Verity's thoughts were racing. She looked at her watch and thought about the seasonal workers they used, realising that without Ralph, it would be impossible to manage with the skeleton staff they had at present.

She spent a frustrating half hour in the office, trying to sort out some additional help, discovering that two of her stalwart, seasonal workers were already employed by The Garden Trug. Just as she was about to close up for the day, there was a knock on the door and Melanie Carson came into the office, followed by her small daughter, Rosie.

'Hi, we've come to beg some parsley.'

'Oh, I'm sure we can find you some, providing Jason hasn't put it all on the compost heap.'

Melanie laughed.

'Is he still proving a trial? Perhaps he's just not suited to the work.'

'Hm, and to top it all, Ralph's leaving. Apparently The Garden Trug offers better pay and conditions.'

Melanie's eyes widened.

'So whatever will you do without him?'

Verity shrugged.

'Oh, we'll manage, no doubt, but it's infuriating all the same. Hiring and firing has always been Dad's province and I can't say I'm looking forward to interviewing.'

They went outside and Rosie went to play with the tabby cat basking in the sunshine. Eventually Verity located the parsley and they went through a wrought-iron gate marked Private, leading to the garden. The early shrub roses were already in bloom, together with the powder-blue ceanothus. As the summer progressed, it would be a mass of colour with a tangle of honeysuckle, jasmine and roses — a real cottage garden.

'Oh, it's so peaceful here!' Melanie said with a sigh.

'D'you want to hear about the adventure I had at lunchtime?' Verity asked her friend.

'Certainly do!'

They sat on the bench overlooking the pond. The two of them had shared secrets since they were Rosie's age. It was Melanie who understood, better than anyone else, what Verity had been through when her boyfriend and business partner had turned out to be deceiving her and their group of friends. He had disappeared into the blue with a substantial sum of their hard-earned capital, leaving them all with a ruined business and copious debts to pay off. Melanie had supported her when the others had given her a hard time, refusing to accept she'd known nothing of what was going on.

'So why didn't you take him up on the offer?' she wanted to know when Verity recounted the incident at March Place. 'Perhaps he was a talent spotter for a local film company!'

'Get real!' Verity protested. 'I was particularly peeved because I was dressed like this.'

Melanie surveyed her friend affectionately.

'Verity, you're a hopeless case. You

don't seem to realise what an attractive girl you are. You've got beautiful bone structure and all that honey-blonde hair! It's a good job I'm not the jealous type.'

Verity laughed, feeling far more relaxed. After Melanie and Rosie had gone, she had a brief word with Ralph, expressing her regret that he was taking a new job, but he merely shrugged and reiterated what he had said previously to her grandfather.

'I think it's high time I paid a visit to the enemy camp,' she told Mr Vernon over supper. 'I need to suss out the opposition and find out how they're managing to filch our customers and workforce.'

At first glance, Verity had to admit that The Garden Trug was very impressive, but she soon realised that this was partly due to the newness of the place. Looking around, she conceded that there were one or two eyecatching displays, indicating that someone had garden design experience.

She knew that she was perfectly capable of producing work like that herself and was aware that, if only her family could afford to smarten things up a bit, then they would present stronger competition. Perhaps it was time to make a few changes at Hollybanks, before it was too late.

Going into the shop, housed in a pagoda-shaped building, she saw that it was about as far removed from Hollybanks as it could possibly be. The central display area consisted of expensive, bought-in hot-house plants, enhanced by a rather ostentatious fountain. She gasped, for leaning against the counter, one arm resting on an enormous photograph album, was the man she had encountered at March Place. He looked up, surprised recognition in his eyes.

'So, we meet again. Have you come to claim your photographs after all? They've turned out rather well, but tell me, how on earth did you know I'd be here this afternoon?'

'Well, you've got a nerve!' she told him crossly for the second time. 'I might have guessed you'd be behind this little outfit. How dare you poach my workforce! And, as for those photographs, I don't know what your game is, Mr Whoever you are, but if you should ever attempt to use them then I'll inform the appropriate authorities!'

There was an amused glint in his eyes.

'Before you make any further allegations perhaps you should get your facts straight. I do not work here, as you mistakenly seem to suppose.'

He extracted some photographs from the folder.

'Here, you might as well have them, as they seem to bother you so much.'

As she snatched the offending snaps from his outstretched hand, her finger-tips brushed his and she felt as if she had received an electric shock.

Verity didn't stop seething until she was halfway back to Hollybanks. Could he have known her identity prior to her visit to The Garden Trug? She realised that, even if she had got the prints, he would still have the negatives. Perhaps she shouldn't have been so hasty and then she would have discovered his intentions, honourable or otherwise.

Fortunately, there were a few enquiries to the job advert Verity had placed in The Kent Messenger, so she arranged to interview the candidates.

Bernard Potter appeared to be the answer to a prayer. He was a large, cheerful-looking man in his fifties, recently made redundant from a landscape garden business twenty miles away. He had good references and said he'd be happy to take whatever hours they could offer him.

Of the other applicants, Liam Donahue came with glowing references, but had an elevated opinion of himself and, unfortunately, there was something about him that Verity did not take to. They gave Bernard the post on the spot and told Liam they would let him know the following day.

'I don't think we've got much option, lass,' her grandfather said, as they discussed things over a cup of tea. 'The others weren't up to much.'

'OK, so we'll give Liam a month's trial,' she agreed reluctantly.

Just as she was locking up, Melanie phoned, asking her if she wanted to go out for a meal that evening.

'Verity, our neighbour's offered to sit in with Rosie. Jim's got a friend staying and a foursome would be much better than three.'

Verity tried making excuses, but Melanie was insistent and so, in the end, she gave in, had a quick shower and changed.

For a few hours, Verity forgot the problems at Hollybanks. Jim's friend, Sean Simpson, was good-looking and delightful company. He told her he had just landed himself a job as an estate agent in Tenterden and was looking for a suitable property to rent in the area.

'And so, in the meantime, I'm staying with Mel and Jim. Do you happen to know March Place?'

She looked at him in surprise.

'Don't tell me you want to rent that!'

He laughed.

'If only! The new owner wants to let the lodge, but I'm afraid it's out of my league.'

She raised her eyebrows.

'I had no idea anyone had bought March Place.'

'They haven't. Apparently, he's a nephew of the late Sir Thomas Thornton.'

'How wonderful to find you've inherited somewhere like that,' Melanie put in. 'I didn't realise there were any remaining relatives.'

'I gather he's been working abroad,' Sean told her. 'Personally I think it could prove to be a mixed blessing. It needs a small fortune spending on it, for roof repairs, redecorating and such.'

'But this nephew isn't planning to sell it, is he?' Verity asked anxiously.

Sean smiled at her reassuringly.

'Fortunately, no. His ambition is to

restore the house and grounds to their former glory so that he can open the gardens to the public during the summer months. Verity, why don't you come over and have a look before he takes up residence? I'll sort something out, if you like, and give you a ring.'

Later, when the two women were freshening up in the cloakroom, Melanie said, 'You've made a hit there, Verity. It's obvious Sean likes you.'

Verity coloured and concentrated on her make-up.

'He's very easy to get on with, but it's no good matchmaking, Mel. After what happened, I'm not sure if I'll be able to trust any man ever again.'

'You mustn't judge all men to be like Paul, you know,' Melanie said gently. 'I reckon you're in a bit of a rut at the moment and that a little fun in your life wouldn't come amiss. After all, you're only twenty-eight!'

A tide of emotion swept over Verity and she tossed her head, feeling vulnerable.

'I'm all right, thanks, Melanie. I really do appreciate your concern but . . . '

Melanie grinned.

'You'd prefer me to mind my own business, eh? The thing is, Verity, I'm so happy with Jim that I'd like to think you could find someone, too.'

Verity picked up her bag.

'Well, I certainly intend to take Sean up on his offer to look round the grounds of March Place.'

'I s'pose that's a start. After all, Rome wasn't built in a day!'

It had been a pleasant evening, Verity reflected, as she got ready for bed. Deep down she knew that Melanie was right. It was time to shrug off the past, but it was difficult to forget what had happened. For a couple of years after leaving university, Verity had been extremely happy. After a gap year in Australia, she had been approached by two of her friends about joining them in a business venture. Fired with enthusiasm, they had taken their business plan to the bank and had managed to secure a loan. With the aid of a van and what amounted to little more than a rented lock-up, they had embarked on their garden design enterprise and it had taken off and escalated beyond their wildest expectations.

Then Verity had met Paul Blackwood at a party and had fallen head-over-heels in love with him. Full of charm, he had volunteered to act as their accountant and, before long had persuaded them to let him join them as a partner, saying that he had a number of useful contacts. For several months the business had continued to flourish, and Verity had never been happier, but then their profits had started to evaporate. The others had challenged Paul, accusing him of misappropriating the funds, but there had been no proof and Verity, blinded by her love, had stuck by him, refusing to believe them. Unfortunately, she had been proved wrong and had learned a very bitter lesson.

She was eternally grateful to her

father for putting up the money to pay off their creditors in order to spare her and her friends the indignity of being made bankrupt. The others had decided to quit and start up again in a new direction. Now Verity felt obliged to remain at Hollybanks and work for her father in order to repay him by the only means she could, and that meant putting on hold any plans of her own for the foreseeable future.

Bernie Potter turned out to be an absolute treasure. Verity had to admit that he was every bit as good as Ralph and that he could certainly teach her a thing or two. Liam Donahue, however, was a bad time-keeper and, if the situation didn't improve, then she would have no alternative but to let him go when the month was up.

2

Sean picked Verity up on Sunday afternoon and drove her to March Place. It was a glorious May day and she caught glimpses of bluebells shimmering in the hazy sunshine. The house was on the far side of Oakhurst, situated in an idyllic spot.

'Brings back memories, does it?' Sean asked as they stood in the sitting-room of the lodge, gazing out over the expanse of parkland.

She nodded, a lump in her throat.

'When I was a child, this was the centre of village life. The previous housekeeper was a friend of my grandmother's and lived here in the lodge, but then, after Sir Thomas and Lady Mary died things changed.'

'Everything changes,' he said softly. 'Let's go outside, shall we?'

The grounds had been sadly

neglected and were badly overgrown. Sean saw her expression.

'I understand the groundsman's really only employed to do general maintenance, cut the lawns, clear the paths.'

'There's so much potential here. It would be a wonderful project to restore the gardens to their former glory so that they could be reopened to the public.'

An idea was slowly forming in her mind.

'This new owner, whoever he is, is he likely to be looking for local people to undertake the work in the grounds?'

Sean nodded.

'I should imagine so, he's not the type to let the grass grow.' They laughed at the unintentional pun.

'I expect he's got his own ideas. How do I find out what he wants?'

Sean took her arm.

'Look, don't raise your hopes, Verity. He's a businessman, quite an entrepreneur from what I hear, so he's probably got his own contacts.'

She nodded. It had been a stupid thought, but for a few moments, her mind had been buzzing with ideas, just like the old days. Just then, Sean's mobile phone rang and she could see from his expression that it wasn't good news.

'So sorry, Verity, I'll have to leave you for a short while. A client's desperate to look round a property in the vicinity and there's no-one else available. The girl in the office has rather dropped me in it.'

'No problem,' she assured him. 'I'll just wander round here for a bit.'

'Look, I'll put my neck on the line and leave the key, just in case it rains, and I promise to be back within the hour.'

She pocketed the key and soon became so absorbed in wandering round the grounds that she lost all track of time. Taking a detour, she arrived at the gardens nearest the house. Here, flowers bloomed in a riot of colour, spilling in profusion on to the terrace and growing between the cracks in the paths. She bent to look, her face alive. Presently, a small summerhouse caught her attention and, impulsively, she pushed open the door.

'Do come in!'

Verity nearly jumped out of her skin and stared in amazement as the owner of the voice turned towards her.

'I don't believe it! It's you again! Whatever are you doing here?' she demanded crossly, looking at the man who had taken her photograph among the azaleas.

'I was just about to ask you the same question. We do seem to keep crossing each other's paths, don't we? Tell me, do you make a habit of wandering round other people's gardens?'

'Yes, when I'm invited. The estate agent, who's letting out the lodge, happens to be a friend of mine.'

'Ah, yes, of course, Sean Simpson. I might have guessed. So tell me, young woman, do people take a stroll in your garden?'

She returned his gaze steadily.

'Yes, they very often do. We happen to run a garden centre. Anyway, what makes you think you've got the right to trespass?'

He grinned at her in an infuriating manner and picked up some papers from the bench.

Suddenly uncertain, she asked, 'Do you work for the new owner?'

His eyes flickered.

'In a manner of speaking, yes. So you see I've got more right to be here than you have.'

'Sean should be back soon,' she said a shade too quickly. 'He's had to see a client.'

'And left you all alone? Shame on him! Tell you what, join me for tea on the terrace and then he'll spot us when he comes looking for you. The house-keeper can act as chaperone, if you like.'

She chose to ignore this last remark.

'This, er, Mr Thornton, what's he like?' she asked, interested in spite of herself.

He looked amused.

'Let's see now, how shall I describe him? Forties, tall, broad-shouldered, considered to be quite good-looking by the ladies, I believe. Can be rather overbearing and arrogant. Definitely not your type. Why all the interest?'

She coloured.

'I knew Sir Thomas and Lady Mary and they were a delightful couple. I didn't know they had a nephew.'

'That's because he's lived abroad for a number or years, but he did stay here when he was a boy, probably before your time.'

They had reached the terrace and he told her to make herself comfortable at one of the garden tables and disappeared into the house. Presently, he reappeared carrying a teapot, followed by a tall, rather thin lady carrying a laden tray.

'Mrs Hall, this is Miss — er — I'm sorry, but I didn't catch your name.'

'Vernon, Verity,' she answered somewhat reluctantly.

As Mrs Hall departed, Verity turned to her companion.

'Is Mr Thornton here? Will he mind?'

He laughed.

'He is here and, he doesn't mind. In fact he's delighted to have your company, Vernon Verity.'

'It's you, isn't it? You're Mr Thornton.'

He inclined his head.

'I wondered when you'd make the connection.'

She was angry now.

'Well, you might have said so earlier instead of letting me make such a fool of myself. I think that's despicable!'

She got to her feet.

'Perhaps it would be better if I didn't stay for tea, after all.'

'Please yourself, but Mrs Hall will be disappointed if you don't sample her fruit cake and, as a matter of fact, I was rather interested to learn about the garden centre of yours.'

She sat down again reluctantly.

'Why should it interest you?'

'Oh, just idle curiosity.'

'Hm, now I've got a question for you. Why the photographs?'

'Oh, that's just a hobby of mine. I worked for a photographic shop during my university breaks.'

Over tea, he managed to extract a fair amount of information from her, without giving much away himself.

Eventually she said curiously, 'And what about you, Mr Thornton? What do you do for a living?'

'Oh, I'm a civil engineer by profession.'

She raised her eyebrows.

'Bridges and things?'

'Yes, you've got the idea.'

Impressed, she settled back to admire the view. When she turned to pick up her cup and saucer she caught her host staring at her again.

'As I've told you before, you're very photogenic,' he said unabashed. 'That pink thing you're wearing complements your colouring.'

She concentrated on her tea. The

pink dress that she had chosen to wear that day had been outrageously expensive. She had bought it for a function Paul had taken her to, knowing that he liked her to look good. It was just as well that this particular outfit hadn't dated because she could no longer afford to be fashionable nowadays.

'This place has certainly got a lot of potential,' she remarked tentatively, watching as Mr Thornton carved into a wonderful nut-bestrewn fruit cake. 'I understand you might be needing someone to redesign the gardens.'

'Yes, indeed. I've received a couple of quotes already.'

'Already?'

She tried not to look disappointed.

He shot her a surprised glance.

'But, of course. It's a fairly long-term project so the sooner it gets underway the better. Why? Had you got someone in mind for the work?'

'Myself,' she told him, taking a deep breath.

He raised his eyebrows.

'You! What do you know about garden design and landscaping?

'For your information, I specialised in garden design at college.'

He passed her a piece of cake, his eyes dancing with amusement.

'Really? Well, I'm afraid you're a bit late in the day, Miss Vernon, because I'm very impressed with the plans submitted by The Garden Trug.'

'So that's what you were doing there the other day!'

She might have known they would have muscled in on the act.

'Amongst other things. Of course, I suppose a little healthy competition wouldn't come amiss. Look, why don't you walk around the gardens with me, tell me what you'd have in mind?'

'So that you can get the owner of The Garden Trug to incorporate my ideas in his designs?' she said stonily. 'I wasn't born yesterday, you know. Anyway, here's Sean. I appreciated the tea, Mr Thornton, but now, if you'll excuse me . . .'

Taking no notice, he called out a greeting to Sean who raised his hand and came across.

'Sorry it took so long, Verity. Have you explained you'd like to be involved in the restoration of the gardens?'

She shook her head.

'No point. Mr Thornton's already made up his mind. Anyway, I've enjoyed my look round and had a delightful tea. Please thank Mrs Hall for me, Mr Thornton.'

Mr Thornton extended his hand.

'It's been a pleasure. Sorry we couldn't do business, but I've more or less promised the job to The Garden Trug.'

A thought suddenly crossed her mind, one which had been there for a while, if she were honest.

'What's the name of the man who owns The Garden Trug?'

'Lawson, Brad Lawson.'

She was immensely relieved, for she had imagined that it might have been Dave Hartley, her one-time business partner.

When they parted company, Sean said, 'I'm sorry it's been such a messed-up afternoon, Verity. If you're prepared to give it another go, I promise not to desert you again.'

'I'd like that,' she assured him and was surprised to realise that she meant it.

She was busily transplanting seedlings the next day when her grandfather approached, leaning heavily on his stick, accompanied by the new owner of March Place.

'Mr Thornton was passing this way and thought he'd drop by to introduce himself, so I've invited him to take a look round the place. I'll see if Mrs Jolly can organise some coffee.'

Verity felt at a distinct disadvantage in her grubby overalls and a sweatshirt which had seen better days. She pushed back a stray curl of hair, leaving a dirty smudge on her cheek.

'So what exactly would you like to see?' she asked to cover a rather awkward pause. 'Hollybanks isn't such a sparkling venture as The Garden Trug. For a start, we're a bit off the beaten track here, but we do stock quite a wide variety of shrubs and can always order anything special.'

'I'm just interested generally in garden centres at present,' he told her.

Washing her hands at the outside tap, she was painfully conscious of his presence, but then pride took over and she began a conducted tour, treating him as she would any other visitor, giving him a brief idea of what they stocked, pausing at the greenhouses and finally at the little shop. She tried to visualise what Hollybanks would look like through his eyes, realising it must seem rather ramshackle and rundown after the shining newness of The Garden Trug. She was relieved when Mrs Jolly approached them bearing a laden tray.

Verity led him through an archway into the private garden and to her favourite spot, a small, wooden table and bench placed in a sheltered alcove.

Above them, a wisteria dripped with heavy mauve blooms.

'It's a bit more makeshift than tea on your terrace, but we like it here.'

'It's charming,' he assured her.

Verity poured the coffee into pottery mugs and passed the scones.

'Help yourself to cream and sugar.'

She was extremely aware of the man sitting beside her and wished her grandfather had joined them, but knew he could find it uncomfortable to sit outside at present. After a while, Mr Thornton turned to her.

'Would you mind telling me why, if you've trained to do garden design, you aren't doing just that? Surely you're wasting your talents.'

'Nothing one ever does in life is wasted, Mr Thornton,' she said in a tone that defied him to question her any further.

'May I ask you to reconsider submitting your designs for the new gardens at March Place? Now, before you refuse, take a look at what I had in mind and then, if you decide to go ahead, I promise to give your ideas favourable consideration.'

Producing an envelope from his inside jacket pocket, he placed it on the table. Taken aback, Verity was silent for a moment, wondering what had happened to make him change his mind and then, suddenly angry, she sprang to her feet.

'Why do you always manage to sound so patronising? And why have you decided to approach me, after making it so abundantly clear yesterday that you were well satisfied with The Garden Trug's designs?'

His eyes narrowed and he stood up, too, towering above her.

'You're a difficult woman, Miss Vernon. I've obviously made a mistake in coming here. However, should you change your mind, give me a ring.'

He handed her a business card.

'Thanks for the refreshments and please say goodbye to your grandfather for me.'

Verity stared after him open-mouthed. He was so incredibly arrogant and her first instinct was to have nothing more to do with him and yet the prospect of restoring the gardens at March Place filled her with excitement. She turned the card over in her hand.

'J.T. Thornton,' she noted, wondering idly what the initials stood for.

There was something about the man that made her want to rise to his challenge of transforming the garden, even if just for the pleasure of showing him what she was capable of doing. Somehow he had managed to kindle her imagination. She flipped over the plans, expecting to see a list of requirements but to her surprise, she found a plan of the way the gardens had looked when Sir Thomas and Lady Mary had first laid them out.

Later, whilst she was eating her lunch, she scanned Thornton's notes with interest. He wanted the gardens surrounding March Place to be in keeping with its character, but the rest of the grounds could be developed and landscaped according to the imagination and skill of the architect.

Against her better judgement and for the first time in months, Verity spent the evening drafting out some rough ideas. She knew that in order to do herself justice, she would need to revisit March Place and, on an impulse, rang Sean.

'I knew you wouldn't be able to resist the challenge once you'd seen the gardens again,' he told her delightedly. 'How about Wednesday afternoon? And this time, just to make sure I don't have to dash off in the middle, I'll book you in as a client wanting to take a look at the lodge.'

3

Hollybanks was already beginning to look considerably better now that Bernie Potter had got into his stride. Quite apart from possessing an expert knowledge of plants, he had turned out to be a competent handyman, replacing glass panels and rotting wooden frames.

Surprisingly, he had taken Jason under his wing, and the lad seemed to be settling down. On the other hand, however, Verity was fast discovering that Liam could be a bit of a nuisance. The exasperating thing was that he was quite capable of doing an excellent job when he chose to do so.

She went into the shed and began leafing through some catalogues, but her mind wasn't really on the task. She kept thinking about the garden project and wondering what J. T. Thornton would have to say about her ideas. How she would love to gain the garden contract so that she could show him that she could produce work as good as that of The Garden Trug.

Business was beginning to pick up slowly. The fine weather had brought a steady trickle of customers. There was a knock and Bernie put his head round the door.

'I was thinking, Verity, that a spot of repainting would improve this place a real treat.'

'I'm sure you're right, Bernie, but the problem is prioritising, because so much needs doing round here at present. I'm afraid we can't afford to hire professional decorators.'

His brown eyes twinkled.

'I'm quite a dab hand with a paint brush myself. It wouldn't cost much.'

She only hesitated for a moment, knowing that he was talking sense.

'It's a good suggestion, Bernie. We could always increase your hours on a temporary basis, if you're sure. So when can you make a start?'

His weatherbeaten face creased into a smile.

'Straight away, if you like. I'll see to the paint and stuff.'

They discussed this for a few minutes and, when he had gone, she got out the calculator, knowing that if she consulted her grandfather he was just as likely to veto the whole idea, saying that they had better wait until her parents returned. Now that she had repaid her loan to them, she could afford to pay for the work herself, if necessary.

On Wednesday afternoon, Verity drove to March Place where Sean was waiting for her. There was no sign of Mr Thornton this time and she felt irrationally disappointed.

'So, what did you have in mind?' Sean asked, as they strolled.

'Oh, a traditional English garden effect near to the house, but using specific colours, blue to deep purple, white and green, purple through to red, that sort of thing, and then creating a new rose garden with lots of pergolas and arbours. I'd renovate the fountain, making it a central feature.'

As she spoke, a dreamy look came into her eyes.

'It all sounds very ordinary, but it won't be. Sean, I really can't give all my trade secrets away, not before I've discussed them with Mr Thornton.'

Grinning, he took her arm and led her to a seat beneath an arbour of pale pink roses.

'Thornton's told me he wants to open the gardens by late summer.'

'But that's ridiculous! It would take an army of gardeners just to sort out the flower beds nearest the house. That's a signal for me to pull out.'

'Certainly not! Look, why don't you submit your designs anyway and wait and see what Thornton has to say?'

She frowned.

'But supposing he takes the best of my ideas and details to Lawson to incorporate them into his plan?'

'That's a chance you've got to take. Anyway, what makes you think it's only

Lawson and yourself who're interested in this project? There could well be others involved.'

This was something that hadn't occurred to her. Sean caught her hand.

'I'm afraid I've got to sort out a couple of things for a client before tomorrow, but how about coming out to dinner with me sometime in the near future?'

'I'd like that, Sean,' she told him sincerely and when his arm lightly encircled her waist she didn't shrug it off, although she hoped he wouldn't get too serious.

All the same, it would be good to have a male friend to go out with occasionally, one who shared her interests but, beyond that, she was just not sure. Returning to Hollybanks, she had just settled down to complete a stack of order forms when Liam appeared, looking decidedly put out.

'I want a word with you, Miss Vernon,' he said somewhat belligerently and her heart sank.

'So what's wrong, Liam?'

'Bernie and this painting. I'm ace with a paint brush. If you'd asked me instead of him, I'd have done a good job. What've you got against me? That's what I'd like to know.'

She swallowed, finding his attitude rather menacing and then got a grip on herself.

'Bernie just happened to volunteer first on this occasion, but please feel free to come up with any other ideas.'

She had taken the wind out of his sails and he said reluctantly, 'Well, OK then, but I need every penny I can get, see.'

She nodded, realising that if she got him on her side, perhaps he would prove to be a good ally.

It was a shot in the dark, but she said, 'Do you have any problems at home, Liam? Anything that I can help you with?'

He shook his head, looking distinctly embarrassed and muttering something inaudible, he sidled out of the office.

She didn't know what to make of him and wished she could find out a bit more about his background. That was to be granted sooner than expected when, the following afternoon, a young woman appeared pushing a toddler in a buggy. Liam happened to be working near to where Verity was checking new stock.

'Is this your little sister, Liam?' she asked curiously.

Liam was rocking the buggy to and fro and the child, an angelic-looking girl with a mop of blonde curls and blue eyes, stretched up small arms.

'Daddy!'

'She's me daughter, so now you know why I need all the extra cash I can get! Cheryl here's me sister. She's brought me lunch.'

Verity was taken aback, but only for a minute and she hurriedly covered her surprise.

'And your partner?'

But he had said enough and, ignoring the question, took the small girl from the buggy and began talking to her softly. Suddenly Verity saw Liam in a totally new light. Shortly afterwards, Sean rang up to arrange their dinner date for Saturday. They chatted for a few moments and then she went back to her rather tedious job with a spring in her step.

The following morning, after delivering some orders, she decided to stop off at March Place. There was a sophisticated new entry system and, after explaining her business, the gate was eventually opened by an elderly man with a rather mournful expression.

Even though the grounds had been sadly neglected, they were still beautiful. The azaleas and rhododendrons, although past their best, were still blooming. Verity realised what a mammoth undertaking it would be to transform the gardens into what she had in mind, but she had to admit that the project excited her. Nearer to the house, the grass had recently been cut and the hedges clipped, giving a better idea of the shape of the gardens.

Verity took a deep breath, realising what a privilege it would be to work here. It occurred to her then that she might have got it all wrong. Perhaps Mr Thornton had no intention of engaging the garden centre submitting the best designs to actually carry out the work. That would be a pity and not nearly so rewarding, but she realised it was a distinct possibility that he might want to employ his own workforce.

She spent the next half hour or so wandering about with her notebook, examining plants and shrubs and sketching in the shape and position of the flower beds so that she could work more accurately on her designs. She was stooping to inspect a very fine specimen of a lily when she heard a familiar voice behind her.

'So, I see you couldn't keep away!'

Startled, she stepped back against Mr Thornton's rather large frame. An arm shot out to steady her and, rather breathlessly she said, 'You shouldn't creep up on people like that.'

He laughed.

'Do I take it you've come to take another look round the gardens for a purpose? Perhaps you've reconsidered my suggestion about submitting your designs, after all.'

She nodded, aware that her heart was beating wildly and that the warmth of his body against hers had awakened emotions which she had no longer believed she possessed. He was, after all, a very attractive man with thick, beautifully cut brown hair and those unusual green eyes which were surveying her in a rather amused manner. She stepped back a few paces, uncomfortably aware that the contrast between their attire was amusing. He was dressed in a pale grey suit, obviously tailor made, whilst she was wearing denims and a rather baggy sweatshirt. Her unruly hair was untidy as usual, and her hands were dirty from grubbing about in the flowerbeds.

'So, have you brought your designs with you?'

'No. They're not quite finished yet.'

'Well, at least I've got you to admit you've made a start on them then!' he said triumphantly.

She was annoyed that he'd caught her out and said reluctantly, 'It's only a rough draft.'

'Naturally. I expect this is new territory for you, isn't it?'

'No, why should it be? I've done this sort of thing before.'

She didn't meet his gaze because this was not the truth. She had never attempted anything on this scale before. It wasn't just a question of working on a few flower beds and landscaping some trees and shrubs. There was so much more and, perhaps she was being too ambitious, but she had absolutely no intention of admitting this to anyone other than herself.

He glanced at his watch.

'Look, it's lunchtime. I'm hungry and suspect you are, too, so how about discussing this in a civilised fashion over a meal?'

Before she could refuse, he had taken her by the arm and propelled her up the steps and on to the terrace where a table was laid for two. She looked at him in amazement.

'But how did you know I'd stay?'

'Actually, I was already expecting a luncheon guest but she cried off at the last moment.'

Verity felt ridiculously deflated but realised she had asked for this. Thankfully, Mrs Hall appeared at that moment and whisked her off to a cloakroom where she did what she could with her face and hair before rejoining him.

'I'm eating alfresco as much as possible so that Mrs Hall can get on with the unenviable task of setting the rooms to rights,' he told her. She grinned. 'Well, it's just as well we're outside because of the compost.'

'Compost?' he queried, a twinkle in his eye.

'Yes, however much I try there's always a certain amount that lingers, together with a rather earthy smell.'

His lips twitched. 'I can't say I've noticed.'

'Go on — I bet you've never entertained a woman looking like me before!'

He considered her carefully, his gaze travelling slowly over her so that the colour suffused her cheeks and she lowered her eyes.

'There's nothing wrong with the natural look,' he commented and, embarrassed, she realised he probably thought she was being deliberately provocative.

She wondered who his guest was to have been. No doubt a man as good-looking as he was would have countless beautiful females only too willing to keep him company at lunch. She was fully aware that, under practically any other circumstances, she certainly wouldn't have been his first choice.

'So convince me, Verity Vernon,' he said at length. 'Why should I feel that your ideas for my new garden would be any better than those of Brad Lawson or Craig Horton, both of whom have already submitted very realistic and interesting plans?'

'Because I've known this place since childhood,' she told him, 'and I've seen it throughout the seasons. I've attended lots of functions here and got a host of pleasant memories.'

At that point, Mrs Hall appeared with a loaded tray which he took from her, uttering his thanks.

'So, tell me about these plans of yours whilst we're eating,' he prompted.

She outlined her ideas for the colour-themed gardens nearest to the house, making the fountain a focal point and replacing the worn flagstones with authentic paving.

'There would be lots of plants grown for their interesting foliage and colour effects, and a number of pergolas and screens creating depth and interest. I'd have quantities of colourful and unusual shrubs, all staged to come out one after the other. There's a wealth there already, hidden beneath all that dense undergrowth. And did you know there are underground springs? I'd want to make use of them to create several new water features.'

As Verity enthused, her face lit up and Mr Thornton watched with interest, noting again what a very pretty girl she was.

'Of course,' she told him, 'you ought to know that I can't stand gimmicks and so, if it's grottos and things dangling from trees you're after, then you've got the wrong person. Besides, they frighten the birds.'

He inclined his head.

'You have very decided views on things, Miss Vernon. I see garden designers as gentle, sensitive types, but you appear to be quite the reverse, although I'm pleased to note that you care about wildlife.'

'And I suppose you're going to tell

me that Brad Lawson is some soft, wishy-washy creature who drifts about talking of tranquillity gardens and communing with an imaginary goddess of nature!'

To her great annoyance, he laughed.

'What is it with you and Brad Lawson? You obviously have cause to dislike the poor man.'

'Actually, we've never met. It's just that he represents what I dislike,' she pointed out.

He picked up his glass.

'As a matter of fact, I've been very impressed by what I've seen on my visits to The Garden Trug.'

'That would figure. You're obviously two of a kind. Anyway, I don't want to talk about that place.'

She concentrated on her chicken salad, reflecting moodily that her companion was bringing out the worst in her and that she really ought to make more of an effort to get along with him. Presently, enjoying the delicious crème caramel that Mrs Hall had placed in front of her, she supposed that her host must have a fair amount of money to be able to give up his job at a moment's notice. Perhaps he had been left it along with the house. It was surprising that he had inherited March Place rather than his father. She decided that there were a number of unanswered questions concerning J.T. Thornton.

When she had poured the coffee, she turned her chair slightly in order to have a better view of the house. It was quite charming, built in the mid-nineteenth century on the site of a Tudor manor house. Over the years the Kentish ragstone had mellowed and was covered in ivy and Virginia creeper.

'I love this house,' she said with warmth.

He smiled.

'Who wouldn't? It's delightful, isn't it?'

Embarrassed that she had spoken her thoughts aloud, she finished her coffee and got to her feet.

'That was a wonderful lunch. I

usually just make do with a sandwich. Many thanks.'

'My pleasure, oh, and Miss Vernon, I really would be interested in seeing your presentation. Could you let me have it as soon as possible, say within the next few days? It wouldn't be fair to keep the others waiting too long for my answer, would it now?'

'I suppose not,' she conceded.

He extended his hand and she took it somewhat reluctantly. The contact sent a tingling sensation running through her fingers and her heartbeat seemed to quicken. What was it with this man?

As she made her way down the drive, she was filled with sudden optimism and realised that she hadn't felt so enthusiastic about anything for a very long while. She took a deep breath. Perhaps her life was about to take on a new dimension.

4

The Italian restaurant Sean took her to on Saturday proved to be a good choice and she felt relaxed. He was a charming companion, witty and entertaining.

They were halfway through their meal when the far door opened and the new owner of March Place entered, accompanied by a lovely young woman who looked like a fashion model. She was slim with long, dark hair and was wearing an outfit which almost certainly boasted a designer label. Sean followed Verity's gaze and raised his eyebrows.

'I wonder who she is!'

Verity was wondering that herself, probably the guest Mr Thornton had been expecting to join him for lunch on Wednesday. It was an enjoyable meal, but she found herself looking rather too often in the direction of the couple at the far table and hoped Sean hadn't noticed. She was glad when, immediately after coffee, he suggested they left to go dancing.

As Verity passed Mr Thornton's table, his eyes met hers. He inclined his head slightly but carried on talking to his companion, who laughed prettily at some joke he had made.

Sean took Verity to a newly-opened nightclub which was not really her scene. Fortunately, Sean wasn't impressed with the place either and so, after a short while, he drove her back to Hollybanks where he gave her a chaste good-night kiss before departing.

Next afternoon, Verity was just putting the finishing touches to her presentation when Melanie and Rosie arrived, ostensibly to buy some bedding plants. It was obvious, however, that Melanie was dying to know how Verity's date with Sean had worked out and so, leaving Grandpa in charge of Rosie, they went outside where Verity gave her friend an edited account of the previous evening!

At the mention of Mr Thornton and his lady friend, Melanie said, 'That guy certainly gets around. He was at the Barnes' dinner party the other evening. Good-looking bloke, isn't he?'

Verity ignored this remark and sent Melanie off in the direction of the bedding plants. She was just rearranging some pots of herbs when none other than J.T. Thornton and the dark-haired woman appeared.

'We were out for a drive and thought we'd call by,' he said to Verity and turned to his companion. 'Tara, this is Verity Vernon. Miss Vernon, Tara Fraser-Ellis.'

The two women exchanged cool, polite greetings and Miss Fraser-Ellis, elegant in a cream two-piece and silk blouse, eyed Verity up and down, as if taking in every detail of her appearance.

'I'm going to be away for a few days and thought if your presentation was ready, I could collect it,' Thornton said.

'Yes, I suppose it is more or less finished, although I had expected to be given a little more time. I'll just go and fetch it.'

Rosie and Grandpa were in the kitchen, eating ice cream. Verity had to laugh when the little girl looked up because she had a chocolate moustache. Hurriedly sweeping her presentation into a folder, Verity mopped Rosie's face and, taking her by the hand, went back to the visitors. Tara Fraser-Ellis had wandered off to look at some planters and Melanie was deep in conversation with Mr Thornton. Rosie rushed up to him, eager to find out who he was.

'Hello, I'm Rosie. What's your name?'

He bent down to the child's level.

'Mr Thornton, but my friends call me Jake.'

'Is Mummy a friend?'

He nodded gravely.

'And Aunty Verity?'

'Hardly. I call him Mr Thornton,'

Verity said matter-of-factly, making him laugh.

Tara Fraser-Ellis appeared and said impatiently, 'Come on, Jake, we don't want to be late for the Donaldsons.'

But Jake Thornton wasn't to be hurried.

'Oh, we've got plenty of time. I just want to purchase some of these herbs for the kitchen garden.'

'I'll wait in the car,' she told him abruptly, and, snatching up the keys, strode away.

Verity avoided Melanie's gaze. She saw to her satisfaction that although Jake Thornton was outwardly calm, his eyes were smouldering with suppressed anger. Melanie covered an awkward moment in her usual diplomatic way, by saying her goodbyes and rounding up Rosie.

Jake Thornton followed Verity into the shop to make his purchases.

'I promise I won't keep you waiting too long for my decision on your presentation. Goodbye for now, Miss Vernon.'

Over the next few days, life settled into its usual pattern. Although the routine at Hollybanks was not monotonous, it was certainly nothing to set the world on fire. Her life, which once was so exciting and full of promise, now seemed rather dreary. Her thoughts turned to Jake Thornton. Had he taken the lovely Tara away with him, wherever he was going?

Her grandfather came hobbling towards her now, leaning rather heavily on his stick.

'Would you believe it! I've just had a call from The Garden Trug, wanting to know if some of their stuff was delivered to us by mistake this morning.'

Verity said something rather unladylike under her breath. Checking the boxes, she soon found that several of them were indeed labelled for The Garden Trug.

'OK, tell Bernie I'm taking an early lunch break and I'll get over there right away.'

Now that she was actually going to meet her rival, she was suddenly filled with apprehension as she arrived at The Garden Trug. Brad Lawson was nothing like she had imagined him. He was short and thickset and his dark hair was sleeked back from his forehead, plastered in gel. He didn't shake hands, just strolled over to the back of the van and, after checking the contents, muttered a brief thanks, then detailed a surly-looking man hovering in the background to unload it.

'Perhaps you'd care to ring the supplier whilst I'm here. It's their mistake and they ought to be told about it,' Verity pointed out.

Brad Lawson shrugged.

'I've just discovered we've got a couple of cartons belonging to you, so perhaps you'd better contact them yourself.'

Ushering her inside, he led her to a small office at the back of the shop where he pointed to a couple of boxes full of garden ornaments. She looked at the invoice which she had stuffed in her pocket and frowned.

'You're right, they are listed as ours, but I can't imagine how we've come to order them. How very curious!'

She supposed her grandfather had decided to try out a new line.

'Perhaps you wrote the wrong code by mistake,' he suggested in a patronising tone, crossing to the percolator, where he poured two coffees, without asking her if she wanted one, and placed them on the desk. 'Now, Miss Vernon, shall we dispense with pleasantries and get down to the real business?'

Startled, she saw the ugly expression on his face and suddenly felt vulnerable in the confines of the small office.

'You've elbowed your way into the garden project at March Place, haven't you?'

She stared at him in surprise.

'As I understood it, the project has not been commissioned and so anyone is free to submit a plan.'

His face darkened with temper.

'My partner and I have been working together on this project for weeks now. We approached Jake Thornton with our ideas long before you showed any interest.'

She returned his gaze unwaveringly.

'That's interesting. I understood he approached you.'

Brad Lawson banged his fist on the desk, making the cups rattle.

'Well, little lady, I intend to get this contract, regardless of what you thought you understood.'

Verity was determined not to give into bullyboy tactics. Just then the door opened and an attractive, auburn-haired woman came into the office. She stopped short at the sight of Verity who stared back at her in utter disbelief. Of her three former partners from the landscape gardening business, the one she had least expected to see here in Oakhurst was Felicity Felton.

'Well, well!' she exclaimed. 'I wondered when you'd show up. Have you had a good look round? If so you'll have realised you won't be able to ruin this enterprise like you did the last one.'

'Felicity!' Verity implored, aware that Brad Lawson was watching the scene with interest. 'Please listen. You've never given me a chance to tell you my side of the story.'

Felicity had a temperament to match her hair.

'Why should I?' she demanded bitterly. 'David and I were left high and dry without a job, whilst you managed to feather your nest very nicely.'

Scarlet, Verity turned to Brad Lawson.

'I don't know how much Felicity's told you about what happened, but I can assure you it was none of my doing.'

'That's what they all say, isn't it? From what I hear of it, you should consider yourself lucky you didn't end up in police custody.'

She swallowed hard and turned back to Felicity.

'My parents paid off our debts, you must have known that. It wasn't my fault that Paul . . . that things turned out the way they did, but I took full responsibility and straightened out our affairs. If you imagined I pocketed any of that missing money then you're very much mistaken. If only you'd kept in touch I could have tried to make amends.'

Felicity stood her ground, convinced she had been a victim whilst Verity had somehow managed to escape unscathed.

'It was your problem, Verity. You were the one who persuaded us to take Paul into the business, so you were responsible when he messed up.'

Brad Lawson opened the office door.

'I think, ladies, if you're intent on continuing this argument then it ought to be somewhere less public. I'll get one of the men to load those boxes into your van, and I think the least you can do, in the circumstances, would be to let Felicity and me have the contract for March Place.'

Verity ignored him.

'So tell me, why did you choose to come here, Fliss?'

Felicity's brown eyes flashed.

'I stayed with you and your family a few times, or have you forgotten that? I like Oakhurst and could see the potential for another garden centre round here. Of course, The Garden Trug caters for a more upmarket type of customer than Hollybanks, but each to his own! And now we've got the opportunity to make a name for ourselves at March Place and we're certainly not going to let anyone stand in our way, particularly not you!'

Verity was stunned that her one-time friend could be so hateful. She made a final plea.

'Please, Felicity, give me a chance to set things straight between us.'

But it fell on deaf ears as Felicity stormed out of the office. Brad Lawson spread his hands in a gesture of indifference and then held the door open for Verity to leave.

As she drove back to Hollybanks, she was miserably aware that the safe, secure little world she had created for herself over the past two and a half years was now well and truly shattered!

Over the next few days, Verity threw herself vigorously into her work at Hollybanks. She had no intention of giving up her chance of winning the garden contract just because Brad Lawson and Felicity were trying to intimidate her.

Verity had no idea what had become of Paul Blackwood after he had disappeared into the blue that night, leaving behind him mayhem for the rest of them to sort out. Deep down, she knew there was no justification for her to feel so incredibly guilty. She had accepted responsibility because she had introduced Paul to the others, but they made the final decision as to whether or not he had joined the business. When Paul had absconded with their takings, it had seemed that closing down the business and paying off their creditors was by far the most sensible thing to do. Much of the garden machinery had been on credit and had to be returned when they discovered Paul had not kept up the repayments. Also, he had taken their one main asset, the van, and without that and the confidence of their suppliers, there had seemed little point in continuing.

As soon as it was possible, the business had been wound up and the three of them had parted company. Verity had attempted to keep in touch with both Dave and Felicity, but her letters had remained unanswered.

Sean phoned during the week, asking if they could meet up for a meal. This time, he took her to a quiet country pub and over the meal he told her he had found a flat and wondered if she would come and take a look at it with him.

'I thought you were supposed to be the estate agent!' she teased.

'Oh, I'm not buying, not at the

moment, at any rate. This is rented accommodation. After all, I can't go on staying with Mel and Jim for ever.'

It suddenly occurred to Verity that, although Sean was always willing to talk about his work, he had never told her much about his personal life, any more than she had mentioned hers.

'Tell me, Sean, have you got any family?' she asked in a bid to find out something more about him.

'Two brothers, both happily married and living in the Midlands. I'm the youngest, still footloose and fancy free.'

'Since when?' she asked so casually that he fell into the trap.

'Since Christmas when I . . . '

He looked uncomfortable.

'Look, I don't want to discuss my past relationships or I might feel I have to ask you about yours.'

Startled, she wondered if Mel had dropped any hints about Paul, but they spent the rest of the evening discussing films they had seen and generally setting the world to rights. When they parted company he kissed her rather awkwardly.

'Just a thank-you for tonight,' he told her lightly.

Theirs was a pleasant sort of relationship, she considered, with no strings attached, which was probably the easiest, as both of them were recovering from past relationships. Seeing Felicity had brought all sorts of memories flooding back, because for a short time, Verity and Paul had been good together, but it just wasn't meant to be.

On Thursday afternoon, Jake Thornton called by, just as Verity was dealing with a minor crisis in one of the greenhouses.

'I came to talk to you about the garden project, but can see that now isn't a good time. Supposing I pick you up around eight and we go for a quiet drink somewhere?'

She didn't want to appear too eager and had a ready-made excuse, because she'd just made an arrangement over the phone with Sean to view his flat that evening. She hesitated.

'Well, I've got a prior engagement, but if you can make it an hour later.'

'All right, nine o'clock it is then.'

Sean wasn't too pleased to learn that his evening with Verity was going to be cut short, but he brightened up when she enthused over the spacious, furnished flat in the large Edwardian house.

'Go for it before someone else snatches it up,' she advised him.

'If I did take it there would be one or two changes I'd like to make. I don't suppose . . . '

He gave her a meaningful look and she grinned.

'Yes, of course I'll help. Now, I've got to get back for Jake Thornton.'

Sean said something rude under his breath, and she rebuked him.

'It was your idea I went ahead with this presentation remember!'

He chuckled and took her hand.

'So it was! Anyway, thanks for

coming over, Verity. You're a star!'

Jake Thornton took her to a quiet inn out in the country and, placing a glass of white wine in front of her, said pleasantly, 'I'll come straight to the point. I liked your presentation. You've got some original ideas and they're a distinct possibility for March Place. However, I also like the other two proposals and so I've got a proposition to make.'

She stared at him, wondering what on earth he was about to say.

'Go on, I'm listening.'

'There's enough work for all three of you. I don't particularly like the idea of contracting the work out, so I'd be happy for you all to co-operate together. That way I could just hire some additional folk to work under your direction and . . . '

He trailed off as he saw the look of incredulity on her face.

'You surely didn't think you could undertake such a large operation on your own, did you?' he inquired.

Her mouth was dry and getting to her feet she said dully, 'I'm sorry, Mr Thornton. I'm afraid I've been wasting your time, after all. Perhaps you could drive me home.'

It was his turn to look startled as he wondered whatever had made her react like that.

'You disappoint me, Miss Vernon. Perhaps you've got cold feet because you don't feel capable of carrying out the work involved.'

She replied icily, 'You underestimate me, Mr Thornton. I can always rise to a challenge, but I'm afraid it would be impossible for me to work alongside the people from The Garden Trug.'

Jake Thornton could not hide his exasperation, drumming his fingers on the table top.

'I think I deserve some kind of explanation. Something's obviously happened whilst I've been away, hasn't it?'

'Yes, I've changed my mind, that's all. Give the contract to Brad Lawson and forget that I ever showed an interest.'

'Sit down!' he said commandingly and she obeyed, realising that she was suddenly feeling strangely light-headed.

He surveyed her pale face.

'Have you eaten?'

She shook her head, thinking that this was the last thing she had expected him to say.

'The least you can do is have dinner with me then I'll drive you home.'

She had no alternative but to agree and over a lovely meal, she relaxed enough to allow him to reopen the subject of the garden project.

'If you'll just hear me out then I'll try to explain. The folk at The Garden Trug are interested in the more elaborate type of garden design, such as an Italian water garden. On the other hand, Craig Horton, the other contender, is passionately fond of roses and just wants to concentrate on the re-development of the rose garden.'

She was interested, in spite of herself.

'I see, so what exactly does that leave for me?'

Her hands were resting on the table and he placed his over them, sending an unexpected shiver down her spine.

'For you, Verity Vernon, I've left the best of all — an old English garden in memory of my aunt, to be called The Lady Mary Thornton Garden. How she would have loved your idea for the pastel garden, colour themed from white through pinks, lavenders and blues, with the restored fountain in the middle, and the arbours with summer jasmine and honeysuckle climbing up them.'

Her large eyes lit up as he spoke.

'You liked it? I wasn't sure if it was what you wanted.'

'It's simple, but effective. I liked the notion of the willow screens and hidden seating areas and the different-coloured foliage to add additional interest. So, won't you please reconsider?'

Her mind was in turmoil as she realised that she would enjoy working for this man and having the opportunity of showing him just what she was capable of doing. However, she still had her doubts.

'I was told you wanted to open in late summer and that's not going to be possible, unless you take short cuts which I'm not sure I'm prepared to do,' she pointed out.

'I don't know who told you that. The re-development of the gardens is important to me and I don't want things rushed. I'll be disappointed if you let me down, Verity, because I happen to think your designs show real potential. Of course, if you decided to join the team then I'd want you to start work as soon as possible.'

'I'd need time to think things over,' she told him uncertainly. 'I promise to give you my answer in a day or two, but I'd have to discuss it with my grandfather first.'

Her parents would be back shortly and she felt certain that she'd get their support. After all, being involved in the garden project would be quite an accolade for Hollybanks.

'Yes, of course. I realise you have other priorities to consider. When are your parents due back?'

'In around three week's time, after my cousin's wedding.'

'Well, I obviously can't hang on indefinitely. Let me know your decision as soon as possible and then we'll need to have a meeting with everyone.'

She didn't want that, but realised it was inevitable if they were to work together as a team and surely Brad Lawson and Felicity could hardly object to her taking part in the project, if they were each to be given their own particular areas to develop. Over dessert, she said, 'You should see March Place in early spring. It's a picture. Redeveloping the gardens will be such an exciting challenge.'

Her eyes shone as she enthused and, not for the first time, he thought what an attractive young woman she was. Tonight she had exchanged the denim overalls for a denim skirt and a white top that made her look about eighteen. He realised that it made a refreshing change to be with someone so totally unsophisticated, but couldn't help wondering what she would look like if she were to dress up in expensive clothes, for a special function.

Verity declined coffee and, shortly afterwards, he drove her back to Hollybanks. She lay awake for a long time that night, mulling over the events of the evening.

A couple of days later, just when she was debating about the best time to ring Jake Thornton and accept his offer, the phone rang. To her surprise, it was Felicity Felton wanting to know if she could come over to Hollybanks, as there was something she needed to discuss with Verity. Reluctantly, Verity agreed and then spent the rest of the day wondering what on earth Felicity wanted to see her about.

Felicity turned up at precisely four o'clock, looking cool and elegant. She greeted Grandpa like a long-lost friend and was charm itself. Presently, however, the old gentleman went off to hold the fort in the office and Verity took the tea into the garden, pretending it was just like old times, and knowing full well that it wasn't. Eventually, Felicity came to the point.

'Have you reached a decision about the March Place garden development?'

'Yes. I liked what Mr Thornton had to say when we met up recently, and I've decided to accept his proposal.'

Felicity's jaw dropped slightly.

'You've seen Jake Thornton already?'

'Yes, a couple of days ago. I assume he's spoken with you, too.'

'Well, of course, he has. He was extremely impressed with our designs, said they were brilliant! I take it he doesn't know about Sussex?'

Verity swallowed hard.

'No, why would he? Personally, I can't see it being of any relevance. We've moved on now, Fliss, started afresh.'

There was an odd expression on Felicity's face.

'Well, I suppose there's no need for me to mention it, if you're not going to be working at March Place.'

So this was the purpose of her visit, was it, to warn her off working at March Place!

'As I've just told you, I've made my mind up to accept the work. Are you threatening me, Fliss?'

'No, of course not! Whatever makes you think that? I'm merely suggesting it might be best if you allowed us to have the entire contract. After all, Jake Thornton's bound to find out what happened between us eventually, isn't he?'

Verity couldn't believe her hears.

'Can't you just forgive and forget, Fliss? What about all the good times we had?'

'You'd like that, wouldn't you, Verity? Just to pretend that it never happened. How do I know you wouldn't pull a stunt like that all over again?'

Verity was angrier than she could remember being for a very long time. She got to her feet.

'I'm going to accept the job Mr Thornton's offered me, and nothing you say or do will make me change my mind.'

Felicity stood up.

'We shall see. Don't think you'll manage to hoodwink Jake Thornton. He's not the gullible type.'

And with that parting shot she left.

Verity decided to ring Jake Thornton right away and accept his offer, before she changed her mind, but all she got was the answerphone so she left a rather garbled message.

For the next few days, she spent every spare moment helping Sean sort out his flat. She didn't pry into his broken relationship, but couldn't help being curious all the same.

'Thanks, Verity,' he said, as they surveyed their efforts. 'I don't know what I'd have done without you.'

She hadn't objected to the arm

resting lightly about her shoulders and then moving to her waist, but suddenly his mood changed and he became more demanding. She pulled away sharply.

'It's been a lovely evening, Sean, but I think we should leave it there. I don't want a heavy relationship and I didn't think you did either.'

'Sorry, I must have misread the signs,' he murmured awkwardly. 'I'll drive you home.'

It was a pity the evening had had to end like that but at least they knew where they stood now. She was beginning to wonder if she would want to be close to any man again, after Paul.

5

On Saturday, Verity decided to go into Tenterden. An invitation had arrived for a buffet supper at March Place, so that all the people involved in the garden project could get to meet one another. Melanie and Jim had been invited, too, together with some other people from the village.

Verity decided she would need a new dress for the occasion. She had had a brief and rather formal telephone conversation with Jake Thornton in response to her message, and it was arranged that she'd begin work on the garden project as soon as it was feasible.

Tenterden was rather a classy little town and the prices in the shops seemed exorbitant. Noticing a sale in a small boutique she went inside and, almost immediately, found a dress she liked in a silky blue material. She was window shopping afterwards when someone touched her on the shoulder. Startled, she turned to find Jake Thornton smiling down at her.

'Sorry, I seem to make a habit of making you jump. I've always had a fancy to go on the Tenterden Steam Railway and I had a free day today. I suppose you wouldn't care to accompany me.'

Surprised, she found herself accepting his invitation and, after leaving her packages in the car, they set off for the station.

'It's a boyhood passion of mine, trains. When I get the upstairs rooms sorted out at March Place I'm going to set up my old train set in one of them. It's very therapeutic, you know.'

'Good for letting off steam!' she teased and he laughed.

He insisted on paying for her ticket on the railway and, as the engine chugged through the picturesque countryside, he said, 'I ought to have brought Rosie.'

She smiled.

'You obviously like children.'

For a brief moment, a slight shadow crossed his face, but was gone again so quickly that she wondered if she'd imagined it.

'Yes, he said shortly and looked out of the window at the passing scenery, giving Verity an opportunity to study him unobserved. She thought again what a good-looking man he was with his lean features, thatch of thick light-brown hair and the hint of a dimple in his chin. He was wearing a pale green, silk shirt and she found herself noting what a muscular body he had. Turning his head, he caught her looking at him and smiled. She smiled back, her dark-blue eyes meeting his grey-green ones.

It was a magical ride, full of nostalgia, as if they were in a time warp, and she wished the afternoon would go on for ever, but like all good things, it eventually came to an end. He helped her off the train with an old-fashioned chivalry and as his hand held hers, she was aware of a magnetism between them which made her catch her breath. She was confused by the intensity of her feelings. Having just managed to convince herself and, hopefully, Sean, that she wasn't ready for another meaningful relationship just yet, she was suddenly overtaken by this unexpected surge of emotion. Jake Thornton — still very much an unknown quantity, had somehow managed to find a way into her heart and she was sure she would regret it.

'Let's have some tea,' he said as they left Tenterden station, 'and then you can tell me what you've got against Felicity Felton, before she does.'

Seeing the expression on her face he explained.

'She dropped rather a large hint when I spoke with her the other day.'

'I don't have anything against Felicity. I'm afraid it's the other way round. She thinks I deceived her. We used to be in business together and we were the best of friends, but something happened to change all that. Look, I'd rather not talk about it. I was just very naïve, misplaced my trust in someone and learned my lesson the hard way. I hope you'll believe me.'

'Why wouldn't I? When the time's right, you can tell me about it, but until then, if asked, I'll say I know already. As long as you've got a clear conscience, then that's all that matters. I also intend to make it perfectly clear that I won't tolerate anti-social behaviour from my workforce.'

She felt as if a great weight had been lifted from her shoulders.

Taking her by the arm, he led her into the nearest café where he ordered an enormous tea. She gradually relaxed, realising that if it hadn't been for Tara Fraser-Ellis then things might have been very different between them. She suddenly felt a pang of jealousy which was out of character for her.

Helping himself to another scone

Jake said casually, 'Going back to the business between you and Felicity, was there some man involved, a relationship you ran away from, perhaps?'

'I don't think that's any concern of yours,' she said tartly and concentrated on her cake which suddenly tasted like sawdust.

'OK, but I'm prepared to listen should you ever wish to talk about it.'

'I'll bear that in mind,' she assured him.

As they parted company he said formally, 'Thanks for your company. See you soon.'

Verity saw him the very next day in church where he was accompanied by Tara Fraser-Ellis, looking lovelier than ever in a cool, apricot silk suit. She was obviously aware that everyone's eyes were upon her as she sat in the front pew beside the new owner of March Place.

Verity had a lengthy chat with Melanie on the phone that evening, finally filling her in with what had happened between herself and Sean. There was a pause before Melanie responded.

'Perhaps it was a mistake to introduce you to Sean. I just thought it seemed like a good idea at the time, what with him having had such a rough time with the divorce and everything.'

'Divorce! I'd no idea. I knew he'd just finished a relationship, but didn't realise he'd been married.'

'Would it have made a difference?'

'I'm not sure. I suppose I'd always feel I was second choice, if it became a serious relationship, but there's no danger of that so it's OK. Matchmaking's definitely not your strong point, Mel. He's just not my type.'

She gave a wry smile as she put down the phone, wondering what her type was exactly. Jake Thornton came into her mind and she realised that compared to him Sean seemed to pale into insignificance. She told herself firmly that she could forget any romantic notions she might have about Jake because he was a rich entrepreneur who already had a ladyfriend, the sultry Tara Fraser-Ellis.

The next few days passed uneventfully at Hollybanks. They were, however, extremely busy due to a spell of uninterrupted sunshine, which sent everyone out to buy plants for the garden. Verity had begun work on a display area at the front of the garden. She was longing for her parents to return so that she could hand over the reigns once more, and concentrate on the work at March Place.

Melanie and Jim drove her to the buffet supper. Jake Thornton had rung up to ask if they could arrive a little earlier, but had neglected to say why. Verity was rather apprehensive but was determined not to let it show. She felt good in the new blue dress and had taken great pains with her appearance. She was surprised to find Jake Thornton standing alone on the terrace, looking immaculate in dark trousers and a cream jacket. Of Tara Fraser-Ellis there was no sign. He smiled at her in a disarming manner.

'I've asked you to come early hoping you'd help me greet my guests and generally act as hostess. After all, you probably know most of them far better than I do.'

'Would you like me to take them on a guided tour of the house as well?' she asked cuttingly and then, as she saw his rather startled expression, was immediately contrite.

'I'm sorry. I wasn't expecting to stand in for Tara.'

There, it was out now and, judging from the grim set to his jaw, she realised she'd said too much.

'Don't worry, you're not but if you'd rather . . . '

At that moment, Felicity appeared with Brad Lawson, and Verity managed a rather fixed smile as she reluctantly took her place beside Jake Thornton. Felicity, looking stunning in a clinging, pale green dress, gave Verity a look which spoke volumes before turning her charm on Jake. Later, as Verity mingled with the guests, Felicity came to join her.

'You're not wasting any time, getting your way into Jake Thornton's good books. You haven't told him about Sussex yet, have you?'

Verity felt her stomach churn.

'Of course I have. Ask him if you don't believe me. If you must know, Tara couldn't make it tonight, which is why Mr Thornton asked me to act as hostess as I happen to know most of his guests.'

'You would have done better to have taken my advice and left this project well alone, believe me.'

Verity was determined not to let the other girl rattle her. Fortunately, Sean arrived just then so Verity introduced them and the next moment they had taken their drinks out on to the terrace and were laughing together.

'That was a clever move,' Melanie said in her ear, 'palming Sean off with Felicity.'

'Not really, as she's with Brad Lawson.'

Melanie's eyes widened.

'Then that's news to me. I know they came together, but I understood it was purely a business relationship.'

Suddenly things seemed more confused than ever. Probably, at that very moment, Felicity was telling Sean everything about Sussex. Presently, Verity slipped into an adjacent room to take a look at the garden plans.

'So what d'you think?' Jake asked, suddenly appearing beside her.

'They're interesting,' she conceded. 'There's a good balance.'

'Yes, that's exactly what I wanted, lots of variety and contrast, too. So, how long do you think it will be before you can make a start?'

'Give me a couple of weeks to sort myself out,' she told him rashly.

'Right, I'll hold you to that!' he said and gave her a devastating smile. 'So how do you like this room now it's been redecorated?'

They were in the garden room at the rear of the house, which had huge windows overlooking the grounds. It had been tastefully redecorated and above the marble fireplace was a striking portrait of Sir Thomas and Lady Mary Thornton and in the hearth stood a magnificent floral arrangement in tones of yellow and cream to match the surroundings.

'It's fabulous,' she said sincerely. 'Melanie tells me you plan to use it for concerts and wedding receptions.'

He nodded.

'I've tried not to alter things too much, but there are a couple of rooms on the next floor that I plan to have refurbished as conference rooms.'

'I'd no idea you were intending to use March Place for that type of business venture.'

'My dear Miss Vernon, owning a house like this is a very expensive hobby and the only way for it to survive is to utilise it.'

She gave a sudden smile, realising

when she was beaten.

'I suppose so. It's certainly better than letting the place fall into disrepair, as it was in danger of doing.'

'I've a good interior designer, and thank you for your support this evening, Verity. You're looking absolutely charming. You should dress up more often.'

Almost before she realised what was happening, he had caught her round the waist and delivered a kiss on her mouth that sent her senses reeling. Suddenly the phone began to ring and, with a sigh, he released her. Watching his face and seeing his smile, she knew it was Tara. After a few minutes, he rang off.

'Tara,' he said, 'ringing all the way from Paris to find out how the evening's going.'

Any romantic thoughts Verity might have been harbouring about him were immediately shattered. The kiss was a thank-you for her support and was not intended to be taken seriously. Tara was unavailable, so she had stepped briefly into her shoes, and, now that he'd been reminded of the beautiful brunette, he'd dismissed Verity as if she were a paid help. And that, she told herself sternly, was exactly what she was.

As the party began to break up, Verity felt there was really no need for her to remain but Jake said, 'If you could just stay until after everyone's gone then I'll drive you back to Hollybanks.'

When the last of the guests had departed and Mrs Hall and her team of workers had begun to clear away the remains of the buffet, he turned to Verity with a smile.

'It's time I thanked you for your support this evening.'

'You already did,' she told him rather breathlessly.

'Oh, that!' he said airily. 'You're looking quite enchanting and it was my way of letting you know.'

'I see. So were you happy with the way the evening went?'

'Yes, I've made some interesting

contacts and found most people to be very supportive. I think it was a success, don't you?'

She had to agree that it had been. During the short drive to Hollybanks, he made very little conversation and Verity, full of her own thoughts, was glad. She knew that she was attracted to Jake Thornton, but some instinct told her to be on her guard. He insisted upon getting out of the car and walking up to the house with her.

There were lights blazing everywhere and immediately she felt uneasy.

'That's odd. Grandpa's usually in bed by now. I wonder if he's unwell?'

The back door was open and, with a sense of foreboding, she went racing up the stairs, but he was nowhere to be found. Jake Thornton had followed her.

'We'd best check the garden centre,' he said tersely. 'Have you got a torch?'

She picked up the flashlight by the back door and, as they went outside again, the cat came rushing to greet them, miaowing in an agitated manner.

The gate leading to the garden centre was wide open and a scene of devastation met their eyes as they went through. They realised that the far greenhouse, containing the more expensive stock, had been broken into and the door was hanging on its hinges.

They found her grandfather lying on the floor, blood flowing from a deep gash on his forehead. She kneeled beside him, stroking his gnarled hand. His eyes fluttered open.

'I knew you'd come, lass. Tried to stop them but . . . '

'Don't talk, Grandpa. Mr Thornton will stay with you whilst I get help.'

But Jake Thornton was already on his mobile asking for the police and ambulance services.

6

Jake and Verity eventually returned to Hollybanks around dawn. Grandpa had been kept in hospital overnight, because he had slight concussion and a head wound, but the doctor had assured Verity that it was nothing to be alarmed about.

'He looks so old and frail. Why on earth would anyone do such a thing?' she asked Jake angrily.

'If it's any consolation, they didn't target your grandfather. Whilst you were giving details to the doctor, your grandfather spoke to me. Seems he tried to apprehend the vandals and tripped over in the greenhouse, hitting his head. He doesn't remember any more.'

'They left him,' she said bitterly. 'Supposing I'd been away overnight.'

'But you weren't, so stop letting your

imagination run riot and let's get some sleep. I'll stop over with you.'

She looked at him, eyes sparkling with unshed tears.

'Oh, but there's really no need.'

'Nonsense. There's not much of the night left and it'll save me waking up the entire household at March Place. They know what's happened. I phoned them after I'd spoken to the police.'

She didn't argue because she was far too weary, but as he came inside with her, reaction set in and she began to tremble uncontrollably. Taking her gently in his arms, he stroked her hair, murmuring comforting words. It took every ounce of self control for her to move away. She made hot drinks, found pillows and a sleeping-bag, and put extra towels in the bathroom and then, thankfully, went to her room. Almost immediately, she fell into a deep and dreamless sleep.

In daylight, the devastation outside became apparent. She bit her lip as she surveyed the scene.

'We'll soon get it cleared up, once the police have finished,' Jake told her, suddenly appearing from behind one of the greenhouses.

Over scrambled eggs and bacon, she realised that in other circumstances she might have quite enjoyed the situation, having Jake there, but all she could think about now was her grandfather lying in hospital, and that her parents had left her in charge during their absence.

As if sensing her thoughts, Jake said, 'He'll be all right.'

She shook her head.

'I phoned just now. He's had a restless night. They want to run tests.'

He took her hand, forcing her to meet his gaze.

'It's not your fault. I didn't want to tell you last night, but whoever it was who did this had a working knowledge of the place, maybe even a key.'

She stared at him incredulously, as his words slowly registered.

'You mean it was an inside job? One

of our workers? But why?'

Just then, there was a knock at the front door. The police had turned up together with some of the workforce and, for the next few hours, Verity was kept busy making copious cups of tea and answering dozens of questions. She had no option but to close the garden centre for at least a couple of days. It would take all of that to straighten out the place and they would have to wait for the loss assessor first.

Watching her employees' reactions, she had realised that, unless they were extremely good actors, they had known nothing about what had happened. Of course, there had been a series of seasonal workers during the past months and there was a key missing when she checked. That afternoon, Verity spent an hour or so with her grandfather who was inclined to be sleepy and rather fractious. She hadn't been back more than half an hour when Melanie turned up to offer help and sympathy.

She was just deciding what to cook for supper when there was a loud knock at the front door. Looking cautiously out of the spyhole, she saw the large frame of Jake Thornton and was delighted to let him in.

'Go and get your glad rags on. I'm taking you out for dinner. No buts. That's an order and I'm used to being obeyed!'

She was too drained to argue, so she went upstairs to change. She selected a simple dark-blue dress from her wardrobe, swept her hair up and lightly made up her face. Snatching up her bag and a white jacket, she made her way downstairs to find Jake sitting in Grandpa's armchair with the cat purring on his knee. It seemed that all the female species liked him!

The restaurant he took her to was quiet, sophisticated and very, very expensive.

'I would recommend the lemon sole,' Jake said helpfully.

He watched her as she enjoyed the

meal, approving of the simplicity of her dress, which enhanced her natural beauty. Compared to her, he thought the other women in the restaurant appeared overdressed and glitzy. She was not like any other girl he had met, much less sophisticated for one thing. He suspected that she wouldn't be happy with a casual relationship and would want a long-term commitment. He was aware that to become involved with her could make things complicated for himself.

She was sampling a raspberry sorbet when he asked, 'Any ideas about who might be responsible for trashing your garden centre?'

'None,' she said shortly, but could sense that he didn't believe her.

She didn't want to discuss it, afraid that someone from her past was aiming to cause trouble for her. Could it be connected with Felicity's sudden appearance on the scene? Looking back, things had started going wrong from the time The

Garden Trug had first opened.

He gave her a searching glance.

'OK, but remember, I'm prepared to listen if ever you want to confide in me. After all, you hinted at something in your past that caused the rift between yourself and Felicity. Could there be a link between that and this recent vandalism?'

'I don't know what to think. What happened was over two years ago and I've tried to put it behind me. Look, I've really enjoyed this meal, but I'm a bit tired and would like to go home now, please.'

To her relief, when they arrived at Hollybanks, he insisted on seeing her inside. She thanked him for an enjoyable evening, assuring him that she would be all right on her own. He gave her a swift peck on the cheek and was gone, leaving her feeling strangely disappointed.

Fortunately, the cleaning-up operation took less time than Verity anticipated. Liam worked like a Trojan, dispelling any ideas she might have had as to whether he could be behind the vandalism. They restored order in a relatively short time, but morale was low when they realised just how much stock had been destroyed. The police finally concluded it had been another case of wanton vandalism.

Verity had no idea when the key had gone missing and there was no proof that it had been an inside job. She had a security check carried out and the locks on the gates were changed, but anything further would need her father's approval. However, they couldn't wait for the insurance money to come through before restocking, which meant that instead of a healthy bank balance, they were now on an overdraft facility which would make her father very cross indeed.

Verity worked frenziedly on her garden display, which mercifully had been left untouched. It was amazing what could be done with some willow fencing, a few paving stones and some coloured gravel.

When she returned later from visiting her grandfather in hospital, she found Felicity waiting for her in the garden centre.

'Verity! Sean's only just told me what's happened! Look, if there's anything I can do to help . . . '

Verity had always known that if Felicity were to offer her an olive branch then she would take it, and, suddenly, she was hugging her friend.

'Oh, Fliss, I can't bear to think of us being enemies. You must know that if only I could put the clock back then I would.'

They went up to the house and sat drinking tea at the kitchen table.

'Do you think it could have been one of your workers?' Felicity asked.

'If it was then I don't know of a motive. No, according to the police, it was probably just an opportunist, although there is a key missing.'

Verity sipped her tea, certain now that Felicity had known nothing about the break-in and she felt ashamed for suspecting that The Garden Thug was involved.

'We should just about be straight by the time my parents return.'

There was something she badly needed to know.

'So tell me, Fliss, how did you come to be involved with Brad Lawson?'

'Oh, he was at university with my cousin, Rob. He wanted to branch out on his own and I said how I liked this area. The next I knew he'd put in a bid for the site and was asking if I'd like to join forces with him. My father loaned me some capital so that I could go into partnership with him, although Brad's family put up most of the money.'

'At first I thought you were his girlfriend,' Verity said.

Felicity laughed.

'No way, although we get on well enough. That's why it's so good you've introduced me to Sean. He's told me you've been out together a couple of times, helped him sort out his flat, but said it was nothing serious.'

'Yes, well, you know me, I like to lend a hand where possible,' she said.

So far as she was concerned, she was pleased about Felicity and Sean.

Felicity got to her feet.

'Well, give me a bell if there's anything I can do to help.'

'Thanks but, fortunately, I've got a good team of workers.'

Grandpa wasn't pleased to find himself confined to the sitting-room once again when he returned home the following morning, but he was looking frail and Verity didn't want any further accidents. Thankfully, when the garden centre reopened, they were able to sell off cheaply some of the stock that had been salvaged and they bought in replacement bedding plants.

On Friday morning, Verity was just putting the finishing touches to her display area, when her parents arrived home.

After greeting her, her father said, 'This place looks wonderful, Verity. It's had a facelift of some kind, hasn't it? But your stock seems a bit depleted.'

Her mother had been admiring her display area.

'It's amazing, darling, and you've have the place freshly painted! But where's Grandad?'

Over an early lunch, her parents listened sympathetically whilst, together, Verity and her grandfather explained what had happened.

When they had finished, her father said, 'My dear girl, you've obviously both had an appalling time, but evidently you've handled it extremely well. Your grandfather has nothing but praise for you!'

A few days later, Verity arrived at March Place to begin work on the garden development. Her father had taken over the reigns at Hollybanks again, commended her on her efficient running of the place and was very supportive of her new venture. He had even agreed to lend her Liam to do some of the initial heavy work.

Jake Thornton met her for a preliminary discussion about the work on her pastel garden. She hadn't set eyes on him since he'd taken her out to dinner the previous week and he was brisk and businesslike.

Verity was impressed by the amount of progress the workforce from The Garden Trug had already made, although it was awkward seeing Ralph again. Craig Horton was making a first-class job of shaping out the rose garden and already Verity could see an amazing transformation.

It was hard-going at first, clearing the ground to find the original framework of the garden and carefully making sure they didn't remove any of the shrubs or plants that were good stock.

During the next couple of days, they got into a routine and soon things began to take shape under her direction. One evening, just as she was winding up for the day, Jake arrived.

'You've worked hard, Verity. It's already shaping up well.'

'It's a bit slow at present, because we want to salvage any existing plants of value. We don't want to be too heavy-handed and regret it later. Liam's discovered a sundial beneath all this undergrowth. That'll clean up a treat.'

'Good. I've looked over the estimates you've submitted and they're well within my budget. The Italian water garden's proving the most expensive.'

He paused and touched her cheek gently.

'You've a smut of dirt right there, your overalls are filthy and your hair's all over the place, but you still look delightful! I wondered if you might care to take a look at Higham Park, near Canterbury on Sunday. They've been reconstructing their garden for a few years now.'

She found herself accepting, aware that she would welcome the opportunity to spend every moment she could in his company.

7

Higham Park was interesting and they were swept up in the owners' enthusiasm, poring over albums of photographs and newspaper cuttings left out for the visitors to browse through. They were entranced by the attractive gardens and filled with admiration for the long-term projects that the two ladies had got in mind. Jake was enthusiastic.

'I particularly wanted to see this place because, although it's on a much grander scale than March Place, it's significant that, without realising it, we've decided to include several of the same features.'

They enjoyed the Italian water garden with its yew hedges; wandered around the sunken rose garden and then took a stroll along the pleached hornbeam walks. Eventually, they found their way into the secret garden, an enchanting spot with a myriad of blooms.

'We must have a secret garden at March Place,' Jake told her and, the next moment he caught her in a tight embrace and, as his lips met hers, she was swept away on an emotional roller coaster.

'You look so pretty I'm afraid I couldn't help myself!' he said.

She gave him a tiny smile, unable to trust herself to speak and, taking her arm in his, they strolled back across the lawns for all the world as if they were a loving couple. She realised it was probably just the enchantment of the secret garden that had made him want to kiss her, but felt the stirring of emotions within her which had lain dormant for some considerable time. Presently, they had a fascinating tour of the Palladian stately home which, so far, had just a few rooms open for concerts and similar functions. It was a wonderfully romantic setting for weddings.

'Both Mozart and Jane Austen are listed amongst the distinguished visitors to Higham,' he informed her and, for a moment, her imagination was fired as she thought of times gone by so that she could almost hear the rustle of silken skirts, laughter and music.

Later, as they approached March Place, Jake said, 'I've just remembered I'm supposed to be dining out tonight. I'm afraid I'll have to get Sam to run you home. It completely slipped my mind.'

As they pulled up outside the house, Tara Fraser-Ellis unwound herself from one of the chairs on the terrace, looking sulky.

'Darling, wherever have you been? I've been waiting ages! We'll be late for the Fawcett-Browns if you don't get a move on.'

Jake said goodbye to Verity and hurried off into the house.

There was silence and then Tara said, 'It won't work, you know.'

Astonished, Verity asked, 'What won't?'

Tara studied her beautifully-manicured nails.

'Oh, don't play the innocent with me. I don't know where you've been this afternoon, but don't get any ideas about becoming romantically involved with Jake. We're practically engaged. He always did have a kind heart and collect waifs and strays.'

Verity was outraged.

'As it happens, Mr Thornton took me to visit a garden this afternoon, but don't worry, I'm not in the habit of stealing other people's men friends.'

She had the satisfaction of seeing Tara looking slightly uncomfortable. From now on, she would make very certain that she kept her relationship with Jake on a strictly professional footing, hard as it might prove to be.

The gardens at March Place looked more inviting with every day that passed. Thornton's groundforce team had worked their socks off, as Felicity so quaintly put it. One hot, July day,

Verity had loaned Liam to Felicity, who needed some advice on the electrics for the Italian water garden. Presently, she decided to take a breather and see how they were getting on. At first, she thought the garden was deserted, but then she saw a tiny figure sitting on the edge of the smallest pond, dangling her feet in. It was Liam's little daughter, Kayley.

Stealthily, Verity crept up behind her, not wishing to startle the child. She caught her round the waist, talking quietly as she did so. Kayley gave Verity a cherubic smile.

'Me paddling!'

'What on earth's going on here? Haven't you got more sense than to allow that child near the water?'

Jake and Tara had appeared from the opposite end of the garden. Shaken, Verity took Kayley by the hand.

'But I've no idea how she came to be here!'

To her astonishment, Tara said, 'It's useless trying to deny it. You obviously hadn't got your mind on things.'

At that juncture, Liam appeared.

'I don't believe this!' he said angrily to Tara. 'I asked you one small favour, to keep an eye on my child for just ten minutes while I sorted something out with Felicity!'

Tara shrugged her shoulders.

'Blame her. She's the one who nearly let her drown!'

Furiously, Verity said, 'Come on, Liam, we'll sort this out on the way back to Hollybanks.'

Verity had never seen Jake looking so angry.

'We need to get to the bottom of this now!'

With Jake Thornton's protests ringing in their ears, they marched off down the drive.

'So, tell me what happened?' Verity demanded, as soon as she could trust herself to speak.

'My mum had to go out unexpectedly, so I had to collect Kayley. I asked Tara if she'd keep an eye on her, just for a few minutes, while I found Felicity to sort something out for tomorrow, and you know the rest.'

Verity pursed her lips.

'So, where exactly did you leave Kayley?'

'Up at the house, playing on the lawn as good as gold, right where Tara could see her while she was drinking her coffee. I was frantic when I couldn't find her.'

'I can imagine. I suppose she must have wandered off. There could have been a tragedy, Liam. We really are going to have to sort something out regarding your child-care arrangements.'

'I know,' he agreed. 'What I don't understand though is why that Fraser-Ellis woman tried to blame you.'

But all at once, it became transparently clear to Verity that Tara had suddenly seen it as a wonderful way of discrediting her in Jake's sight, without having to try very hard, and of shifting the blame away from herself at the same time. Tara had probably been attempting to find Kayley when Jake had appeared on the scene.

It hurt Verity very badly to know that Jake disbelieved her and, suddenly, she realised that it was because she was in love with him!

When she arrived at March Place the following day, she was relieved to learn that Jake was away on a business seminar. She hoped that by the time he returned, the previous day's episode would have been forgotten. Mrs Vernon had arranged that Liam would bring little Kayley over to Hollybanks the very next time he had a problem with finding a child minder.

The willow screens arrived that morning for the Lady Mary Thornton Garden and, once they had been erected, the transformation was amazing. It now only remained for Verity to finish restocking the flowerbeds and to clean up the fountain.

Verity called to see Melanie the next evening. She told her friend most of what had happened between Jake and herself since they had last met up.

'Well, of course, Jake Thornton's a bit like you, you know, neither of you finds it easy to trust people, and you're both as stubborn as mules. Oh, believe me, you are! Don't let that silly Fraser-Ellis woman prevent you from fulfilling your dreams. I think the problem is that you're growing rather too fond of Jake Thornton for her liking!'

'Don't be so ridiculous!' she chided her friend.

'Come on, it's not like you to give up so easily, Verity and, besides, there's masses of work still to be done at March Place.'

'I admit I would have liked to have attempted a secret garden.'

'There you are then. Just so long as Jake can see your work's good, then he's not going to let you go that easily. You've got real talent, Verity. Don't waste it!'

The following day, Verity was on her own, as Liam couldn't be spared from

Hollybanks. She was on her knees, coaxing a newly-acquired summer jasmine to go in the direction she wanted it to, when a familiar voice behind her said, 'I see you've been working miracles whilst I've been away.'

Jake helped her to her feet.

'I think I owe you an apology, Verity Vernon.'

'I've forgotten,' she told him awkwardly, unable to meet his eyes.

'It seems Tara was so afraid something had happened to young Kayley that she panicked and, in the heat of the moment, put the blame on you.'

So that's what she'd told him, was it?

'It's all water under the bridge now,' she said unsteadily. 'I had hoped you'd know me better than that, but obviously not.'

For an answer, he took her hands between his.

'I'm so sorry. Will you forgive me, Verity? I'd like to think we're friends again, so how about coming out to dinner with me tonight?'

'I'm afraid I'm busy tonight and now, if you'll excuse me, I must press on. This jasmine needs a lot of attention.'

He stooped to look at it.

'I'm glad you've chosen jasmine. It's got such a beautiful scent. It reminds me of hot summers and . . . ' He stopped abruptly.

'I'm replacing some of the old stock,' she reminded him, wondering what else he had been about to say.

There were a number of things about Jake Thornton that remained a mystery. She wondered how much Felicity had managed to find out about his background and resolved to ask her. The opportunity arose next day.

'Fancy coming round for supper tonight?' Felicity asked her surprisingly.

Verity agreed readily, glad that they had finally put the past to rest. They watched a video and sat discussing it over a pizza, just as they used to do years back. Disappointingly, when Verity asked about Jake Thornton's background, Felicity knew no more than she did.

'Now it's my turn for a question. Do you really have no idea what became of Paul?' Felicity asked.

'Absolutely none at all. It was an enormous shock to me, too, when he shot off like that.'

'I know that now, but, at the time I believed you were both in it together. D'you think he's gone abroad? Dave's father contacted the police, you know, but they never came up with anything.'

'Yes, I did know because they interviewed me at the time, and, in case you're wondering, I am aware he had a record. The problem was that I was a poor judge of character. I still find it hard to believe Paul could have been so unscrupulous. Sometimes, I don't think I'll ever be able to trust myself in a proper relationship again.'

'But you were so good together and we all worked so well as a team. No-one can take away the good times we all had. It was unkind of me to want to take it out on you, but I was just so angry.'

'So are you in touch with Dave?'

'No. Last I heard, he was in America. Brad knows him slightly.'

'So how much does Brad know?'

'Some, and now he's aware it really wasn't your fault.'

'I'm just relieved it's all behind me. Now I can look to the future.'

She was to remember those words when she turned up at March Place with Liam on Monday morning, for the sight that greeted them was unbelievable. The Italian water garden, the farthest away from the house, had been completely sabotaged. Rocks had been thrown into the ponds, red paint sprayed over the new flagstones, water lilies and plants uprooted. Jake stood with pursed lips in the midst of this sea of destruction, whilst a white-faced Felicity seemed to have been struck dumb.

'I haven't checked with the rest of you,' Jake said grimly.

'Our garden's intact,' Verity told him. 'I don't know about Craig's.'

'Someone's pruned my roses and scattered them everywhere. There are hardly any left untouched!'

'Why?' Jake Thornton echoed everyone else's thoughts. 'Is it someone's idea of a sick joke? I suppose it's possible it's the same vandals who caused such havoc at Hollybanks. Well, the police will have to be notified and I'll need to contact the insurance company. Liam, can you take a scout round, see if there's any sign of where they got in?'

Verity reflected that it was odd that hers was the only garden which hadn't been vandalised. Of course, the simplest explanation was either because it was overlooked from the house or that whoever did it had mistakenly thought the water garden to be Verity's project. She had originally submitted plans for all the areas, as indeed had the others.

8

After all the enquiries had taken place, Jake Thornton had sent everyone home for the remainder of the day, but they all turned up early on the Tuesday to lend a hand to put right the damage. Several hours later, Verity sat on one of the new benches in The Lady Mary Thornton garden, deep in thought. A sigh escaped her.

'Oh, dear, that was heartfelt!'

Startled, she looked up to see Jake smiling down at her.

'Thought you'd be here.'

He sat down beside her, stretching out his long limbs.

'Surely there has to be a reason for such mindless vandalism.'

'Someone with a grudge against garden centres, perhaps?'

'Very probably. Anyway, the police are on the look-out and we'll need to be more vigilant in future.'

She nodded, very conscious of the man beside her. He looked weary and careworn and she longed to comfort him. His eyes met hers.

'Look, I could do with some company. Why don't you come up to the house and join me for dinner?'

Verity laughed and indicated her grubby apparel.

'Like this? Mrs Hall would be shocked. It's kind of you, but my mother's expecting me for dinner.'

'Then I shall have to eat in solitude, unless, of course, we could compromise. What about first and second courses here, pudding and coffee at Hollybanks?' he suggested.

'Now you are being ridiculous!'

In the end, she agreed, much to her mother's amusement and against her own better judgement.

It was a wonderful July evening and they ate dinner on the terrace which overlooked The Lady Mary Thornton Garden. She had changed into a pale apricot dress and brushed her hair until it shone like spun gold. Dinner was tantalisingly delicious, salmon and cucumber mousse followed by noisettes of lamb, served with new potatoes and a mixture of vegetables.

Presently Jake said, 'Perhaps it would make sense if you told me what happened in Sussex, because I can't help suspecting it might have something to do with these latest incidents.'

Her stomach turned over.

'That was over two years ago.'

'The past has a nasty habit of catching up with us when we least expect it to,' he said quietly and, suddenly, she found herself telling him about Paul.

He listened intently.

'He did a vanishing act with our money, the van and most of the expensive equipment. Afterwards, I found out he was known to the police, quite a con man and I felt such a fool.'

There was a frown on Jake's handsome face.

'So why did he bother with your little enterprise, I wonder.'

'Possibly because it gave him a cover for something much larger. That's the conclusion Felicity and I have reached, although the police have never come up with anything specific.'

'And you loved this Paul?' he asked gently.

The hand holding the glass trembled.

'At the time, yes, I suppose I thought I did, but it was probably just an infatuation. He let me believe he and I had something special going for us, perhaps even marriage.'

'And I take it you've never heard from him since,' he said softly.

She shook her head, not trusting herself to speak. He reached out and took her hands in his.

'Do you still care for him?'

She was taken unawares but met his eyes straight on.

'No, I'm trying to forget him. He ruined my life.'

He squeezed her hands.

'Ah, but now you've got a new one here. I'm glad you've told me. Now, let's go and sample the culinary delights at Hollybanks.'

On the way, Verity realised that Jake had managed to extract a great deal of information from her without telling her anything at all about himself.

They spent an enjoyable time at Hollybanks where Jake charmed her mother, spent time with Grandpa, who was keen to show him some particularly special stamps from his prized collection, and showed an intelligent interest in her parents' recent Australian trip.

When he had gone, her mother commented, 'What a gorgeous man!' and watched carefully for her daughter's reaction, but Verity, busying herself with clearing the coffee cups, didn't reply. Nevertheless, her heart was beating rapidly and she found herself imagining a situation where she was certain of his feelings for her. At present, she felt that he had singled her out simply because it suited him to do so whilst Tara was unavailable. After all, he was not to know that Verity would want no more than a casual relationship.

Fortunately, for the next few days, there were no further problems at March Place and things ran smoothly. Verity worked hard to complete the Lady Mary Thornton Garden, knowing it met her expectations and had been a thoroughly rewarding task. The other gardens were coming along well, too, now that the glitches had been sorted out.

Grandpa's youngest brother, Jack, had phoned up wanting to visit whilst his daughter was on holiday. He was a great favourite of Verity's, a widower who lived with his daughter in Essex. This posed a problem for Mrs Vernon, who hadn't a clue where to put him because the previous time he'd stayed, Verity had been in Sussex. Without hesitation, Verity offered to sleep on the put-you-up in the sitting-room, inwardly wishing she had her own flat again.

After a tiring day at March Place, Jake offered to drive her home because Liam had needed the van to do some deliveries for Hollybanks. When they arrived at the house, Mrs Vernon was looking rather harassed and it soon became apparent why, when Uncle Jack, jovial as ever, appeared on the doorway beside her, and gave Verity a hug.

'I had the chance of coming a day early, so I thought I'd give you all a nice surprise.'

Mrs Vernon hustled him into the sitting-room and said in a whisper, 'He did that all right. I don't know whether I'm on my head or my heels. I hate turning you out of your room like this, Verity. Anyway, come and have some tea, Jake. I'm sure you could do with it.'

Over tea, Jake Thornton summed up the situation.

'Of course, there's a very simple explanation that would ease your accommodation problem.'

'I know, build an extension,' Uncle Jack joked.

Jake turned to Verity with a smile.

'How would you feel about moving into the lodge for the duration of your uncle's stay?'

Verity was so taken aback that, for a moment, she didn't reply, and then she realised that all eyes were turned on her.

'It's a very kind offer, Jake, but I really don't mind sleeping on the settee, and my mother might be glad of an additional pair of hands.'

Mrs Vernon laughed.

'You know I can manage perfectly all right. Mrs Jolly will help out. No, you go, Verity. It'll be good for you to have your own space again.'

Verity made a sudden decision.

'All right then, I will. The lodge is a lovely place and it will be good to be on the spot for work.'

Jake looked pleased.

'Good! I'll tell Mrs Hall and arrange for Sam to pick you up in a couple of hours or so. Fortunately, I've had the electricity put back on so it's quite habitable.'

After Jake had gone, Verity wondered if she were doing the right thing. Wouldn't the other members of the team misconstrue the situation, think it was favouritism? Later, surveying her surroundings in the lodge, Verity realised just how privileged she was to be there. It was a delightful old house which had been tastefully modernised. Jake had thoughtfully arranged for Mrs Hall to make up the bed and there was even a vase of flowers on the sitting-room table.

The following morning, it took Verity a few minutes to remember where she was. After an invigorating shower, she dressed and decided to have her breakfast outside. Her mother had given her some essential provisions, and she had promised to stock up later in the day. She was standing at the gate, soaking up the peaceful atmosphere, when Jake appeared dressed casually in jeans and sweatshirt, a young boxer close on his heels.

'Good morning, Verity, breakfast's in ten minutes.'

She was startled.

'Oh, but I wasn't expecting that. My mother's given me some basic provisions.'

Confused, she stooped to pat the dog.

'Let me introduce you. Verity meet Prudence, Prudence this is Verity. She'll be good for security and I promise to keep her away from the gardens. Now, if you'll excuse me, I've letters to post. See you in the breakfast room in around ten minutes.'

The breakfast room had not yet been redecorated but was, nevertheless, quite charming.

'I thought we'd eat here this morning, rather than on the terrace,' Jake told her and she wondered if it were to avoid gossip, should any of his workforce arrive early.

During breakfast, he made very little

conversation, but it was a companionable meal. As she tackled an enormous plateful of bacon, eggs, mushrooms and tomatoes she said, 'It was good of you to let me stay in the lodge, Jake.'

'No problem! As you know, I'd hoped to rent it out, but there hasn't been much interest, so I've asked Sean to withdraw it for the time being.'

A thought suddenly occurred to her.

'Can I . . . that is, were you expecting rent?'

He gave her a withering look.

'Verity, I asked you to stay at the lodge as my guest. If you decide you'd like to remain, after your uncle leaves, then that would be a different matter entirely.'

A slight colour tinged her cheeks, as she wondered if she had offended him. They were lingering over second cups of coffee when he looked at his watch and, with a muttered exclamation, sprang to his feet.

'If you'll excuse me, Verity, I've got some business to attend to. Stay as long as you like.'

Before she could reply, he had gone.

She spent most of the morning trimming the final section of the yew hedge that bordered the Lady Mary Thornton Garden on three sides. It had been a slow, painstaking job because in order to give it a professional look, she had insisted on cutting it back by hand. As they snatched a quarter of an hour for elevenses, Verity wondered if she ought to tell Felicity that she was staying at the lodge, but decided against it for the moment. She'd find out soon enough no doubt!

She wanted to ask Craig his advice about renewing some of the shrub roses, and found him deep in conversation with Brad. She sensed that both men were rather put out to see her. Craig looked distinctly guilty. It wasn't the first time she'd seen them having a pow-wow recently and she wondered what they'd been discussing.

Liam came over that afternoon and

together they managed to get the small water feature working, which proved more difficult than they had anticipated. He then helped her to erect a small seating area and a pergola. They were admiring their handiwork when Jake Thornton appeared.

'That's looking good. Well done, the pair of you!'

He produced his camera and took a few shots.

'As you know, I've been keeping a photographic record so that we can see the progress that's being made. Come on, Liam, how about taking a couple of snaps of Verity and myself?'

Grinning, Liam obliged and, as Jake stood beside her, Verity wished they really were a couple. Afterwards, he indicated the large screen of conifers at the top end of the garden.

'I reckon it would be a good idea to have the secret garden leading off from here, bordering as it does on the wooded area.'

Verity's eyes shone.

'I was so hoping you might suggest that, Jake.'

'Of course, we'd need to consult with the others first, see what they have in mind for the next stage of the development.'

After he had gone, Liam set down the tools he'd been cleaning.

'Well, that puts paid to that then! They're bound to oppose your plans. Don't like sharing the work do they? Brad and Craig are getting thick, always talking together. I reckon they want the contract for themselves so's they can have all the glory!'

Verity stared at him.

'Well, there's plenty of work for everyone, surely.'

Deep down, however, she was aware that Liam was probably right. She was convinced, more than ever now, that something was going on.

Verity would have preferred to have spent a quiet evening at the lodge, but she had promised her mother she'd join them for a meal. Just as she was ready

139

to leave, she saw a familiar car speeding up the drive with Tara Fraser-Ellis behind the wheel, and felt a sharp pang of unaccustomed envy as she imagined the cosy, candlelit dinner they were about to share. Uncle Jack was always good for a laugh, however, and so it was impossible to remain in a sombre mood for long in his company.

The next morning, Verity overslept. It was one of those misty, drizzling days which showed no sign of letting up and so, on a sudden impulse, she decided to go shopping in Tunbridge Wells that morning. She was grateful to her mother for lending her the car for a few days. She supposed she ought to let someone know her plans, but told herself she was a free agent and if she went up to the house, Jake might think she was expecting breakfast again.

After a couple of hours shopping, she ended up stopping for coffee. She had just found a table when, to her surprise, she saw Tara Fraser-Ellis heading towards her.

'Mind if I join you? Jake's doing some business and we've arranged to meet up for lunch.'

Verity could hardly refuse. It seemed she couldn't even enjoy a cup of coffee without the woman popping up. Tara settled herself down.

'I'm going to a summer ball with Jake and can't find a thing to wear. I guess I'll have to take a trip up to London.'

'What a nuisance for you,' Verity mumbled.

'Have you finished your gardening?' Tara asked.

'No, I decided to come shopping because of the rain.'

A tiny smile played around Tara's lips.

'Of course. I hope to be very much more involved from now on. I'll be moving into March Place shortly and I'm going to take over the garden project from Jake.'

'And is this likely to be in the very near future?'

'Just as soon as it can be arranged.'

'But I understood you had business enterprises of your own.'

'Oh, I do, but I can always put someone in charge. You may not know this, but Brad and Craig are going to join forces. That way they'll be in a position to use all the best equipment for large contracts, like March Place, and have twice the workforce. Jake is a shrewd business man and would be foolish not to let them have the contract.'

'Don't you mean the monopoly?' Verity asked in a voice of steel.

Tara's hazel eyes flickered.

'Of course, that's what they had expected in the first place. Anyway, I'm glad I've had this opportunity to put you straight. I wouldn't have wanted to have raised your hopes about further work.'

She glanced at her watch and got to her feet.

'Must dash. I don't want to keep Jake waiting. Goodbye, Verity.'

Suddenly a great many things slotted

into place. On reflection, Verity supposed she had rather pressed to have her plans for the garden project considered. Perhaps Jake Thornton had taken pity on her!

As she drove back, her mind was in a whirl. She was bitterly disappointed that she wouldn't be involved in any more of the garden project and knew she couldn't bear the thought of Tara as mistress of March Place. She was approaching the crossroads, about a mile from the lodge, when, without any warning, the rain sleeted down. For a split second she lost her concentration, so that she had to swerve to avoid an oncoming van and, losing control, she careered across the road and into a ditch.

9

When Jake arrived at the Accident and Emergency department, he found Verity sitting in a cubicle looking forlorn, streaks of blood on her face and clothes. All he wanted to do was gather her into his arms.

'Thank goodness! I've been out of my mind!'

'So what kept you?' she asked crossly and promptly burst into tears.

'I think that's the cue for me to produce a large, snowy-white handkerchief, but I'm afraid you're going to have to make do with a rather crumpled, medium-sized blue one instead. Now, supposing you tell me what happened.'

He took her hand between his and, in spite of her weakened state or maybe because of it, it set her pulse racing.

After she had given him a garbled version of events she said, 'I knew you'd come, but how did you find out what had happened?'

'Sam was taking Prudence for a walk and saw the police car at the cross-roads. He recognised the car in the ditch as yours. The police told him the ambulance had just left and so he phoned me.'

'You were supposed to be having lunch with Tara,' she said.

He gave her a surprised look.

'We'd just been served with our main course when I left her high and dry. Anyway, how did you know about that?'

He sensed she was keeping something back from him. He'd have to have a word with Tara and find out exactly what they had been discussing.

Several hours later, Jake drove Verity back to March Place. She had a couple of stitches in her chin and a few cuts and bruises, but had otherwise escaped miraculously unscathed.

'You're to stay up at the house. It's no use arguing because it's all settled! I've assured your parents you're still in one piece, and your mother says to tell you she'll be here later with your things.'

As memories of the conversation with Tara came flooding back, Verity realised that the very last place she wanted to be just now was March Place, where she'd probably encounter that young woman again. By this time, however, she was far too weary to voice her objections. Presently, after a light supper and a short visit from her mother, she found herself tucked up in a vast bed in one of the many bedrooms, and, to her surprise, had a fairly comfortable night.

The following morning, after breakfast, Jake popped in to see her.

'Well, what a charming picture! Are you comfortable?'

'Perfectly, thank you. I feel a complete fraud! Jake, there are things we need to talk about.'

'I know, but they'll just have to wait for the time-being. You just concentrate on getting well again.'

He gave her a kiss, leaving her

feelings in turmoil all over again.

By the next day, Verity was feeling well enough to spend the morning in the sitting-room at the front of the house. People kept popping in and out and then, towards lunchtime, Tara put in an appearance.

'Well, isn't this cosy? You really know how to turn things to your advantage, don't you? Managing to worm your way first into the lodge and then into this house.'

Verity sat staring out of the window until she realised Tara had taken the hint and left the room. Then Felicity arrived and, after a few moments chatter, Verity said, 'Tell me about this proposed business amalgamation between The Garden Trug and The Rose Centre.'

'That's supposed to be top secret, bearing in mind they haven't even told me yet. I suppose they intend to present it to me as a fait accompli and offer to buy me out, if I don't agree to go along with them. I've only got a thirty per cent share in the business. So, come on, how much do you know?'

And so Verity gave her a brief résumé of the conversation she'd had with Tara on the morning of the accident.

When she had finished, Felicity said, 'Ah, but Tara's missed out a couple of important points. I overheard Brad and Craig discussing things at The Garden Trug about ten days ago. Apparently, Tara's father and older brother are in property development. Craig's centre's on the edge of an area of land they've earmarked for a new housing estate.'

Light began to dawn.

'So, they're buying Craig out at an attractive price.'

'Got it in one! Tara's brother just happens to be friendly with Brad. Tara fancies trying her hand at the garden design business on the management side, so now do you see?'

'I'm not sure. Are you trying to tell me Tara wants to join forces with Brad, too? It seems an unlikely alliance.'

'Oh, come on, Verity! Old man

Fraser-Ellis dotes on Tara, but what she really wants he can't acquire for her. Surely you've guessed by now that she sees herself as Jake Thornton's wife.'

'Oh, yes, I realise that,' she said bleakly. 'Wait a minute! Now I see what you're driving at!'

'Thought you might. If her daddy pours a substantial sum of money into Brad's and Craig's new joint business venture, with the proviso Tara manages any further work here, then I reckon the garden contract will be in the bag, don't you? And Tara will have got a very firm foothold here.'

How Tara must love Jake, if she were prepared to go to such lengths to please him! Verity swallowed hard. The Lady Mary Thornton Garden was almost finished but, in spite of everything, she'd had dreams of staying on. Now Tara was doing everything to prevent that from happening.

'Why does Tara want to ruin everything for me?' she asked bitterly.

'You really don't know? Because she

thinks you pose a threat to her, of course. Come on, Verity, you must realise that Tara won't tolerate competition and she knows that Jake is more than a little interested in you.'

If only Verity could believe that!

'But Tara has everything. She has no cause to be worried about me.'

Felicity gave her a pitying look.

'If you say so. Anyway, now you know as much as I do. I just wonder if Jake's aware of all that's going on.'

'Just tell me one thing. Who do you think was responsible for the vandalism?'

'Now you have me. Perhaps it really was just some mindless individual with a grudge against Jake Thornton. I can't think of any other motive.'

'Well, now you've told me about the proposed merger, I can appreciate why the others don't want me to have any further part in things.'

Verity was left with a great deal to mull over that afternoon.

At the weekend, Jake Thornton

invited Verity's family over for Sunday lunch. Mrs Hall excelled herself and the whole occasion was enjoyed by everyone. Afterwards, they were taken on a tour of the three finished gardens, each quite beautiful in its own individual way. Jake enthused about his proposed ideas for the future development of the grounds.

'And will Verity have the opportunity to do any further work here?' her father asked.

'I sincerely hope so, if she'd like to, of course. We're going to have some meetings shortly to discuss further contracts and such.'

A thrill of excitement ran through Verity at his words, but then she remembered her conversation with Felicity, and realised how impossible things would be once Tara was in charge.

Later that evening, when the Vernons had returned to Hollybanks, Verity received an unexpected visit from Melanie.

'Your mother said you were back in the lodge and I've been dying to take a look. Well, I must say you've got it made here. I wouldn't want to give up this place in a hurry.'

'It might not be that simple.'

She relayed the conversations she had had with both Tara and Felicity.

'It sounds to me as if Tara's all out to get what she wants, at all costs. I suppose you do know Jake Thornton's in the millionaire bracket.'

'He had to be wealthy to be able to afford the upkeep of March Place.'

'Tara's family might be well off, but they don't come from aristocratic stock like Jake, do they? Actually, don't you find it a bit odd that his uncle left March Place to Jake, instead of to his father?'

It was something Verity had wondered about herself. After all, surely by now, one or other of Jake's family would have put in an appearance, if only out of curiosity. She supposed there was probably a simple explanation.

Jake asked to see Verity the very next evening. They went into his study and he asked her rather formally to be seated. It proved to be a disturbing interview. Jake's forehead was furrowed in a frown.

'I'll come straight to the point, Verity. I had hoped that we could work together for several months to come, but I'm afraid that won't be possible now. I thought I knew you well enough by now, Verity, but obviously I'm a poor judge of character.'

Verity was bewildered.

'What is it, Jake? Have I done something to upset you?'

'You've certainly disappointed me!'

His lips were set in a tight line and, for a moment or two, he did not reply. There was a sinking feeling in Verity's stomach. She couldn't begin to imagine what she had done to make him so angry. At last he spoke.

'Tara's just recounted to me what you told her on the morning of your accident, how you'd sooner throw away the chance of being entered for the award, than to work as a team with her and the others on future projects.'

Verity stared at him open-mouthed.

'Tara told you that? And you actually believed her? How could you?'

She felt the colour rising to her cheeks and, head held high, flounced out of the room. Jake stared at the door, realising he'd probably made one of the biggest mistakes of his life. How could he have doubted her integrity? There were things he had to sort out before the situation got completely out of hand.

It wasn't until Verity was back at the lodge, in a dreadful temper, that she remembered what Jake had said about an award and wondered whatever that was all about. She had just made a pot of tea when Liam arrived, clutching her cardigan.

'You left this on the bench, Verity. So, do we go ahead with the secret garden, or what?'

Over tea and biscuits, she told him the gist of what had been said.

'Cor, I'd really like to fix them others!' he exclaimed then seeing her look of alarm he added hastily, 'Just joking, though I might have done it at one time, but now there's Kayley to think about. Tell you what, though, I bet if the boot was on the other foot, then Tara's brother wouldn't think twice about sorting things out for her.'

She stared at him.

'What do you know about her brother, Liam?'

'She's got two brothers. The younger one's been in a bit of trouble, drugs and that, well, the word gets round when you know some of the blokes I do. Of course, his family try to hush it up. Anyhow, I reckon that's how Brad Lawson got to know him. He's supposed to be clean now, but he did a spell inside.'

'Are you telling me that Brad Lawson . . . '

'No, but sometimes it's the ones that are walking the streets that are as guilty as the ones inside. It's a question of who gets caught.'

'Let's get this straight, Liam. You're telling me that Tara Fraser-Ellis's brother has been in prison and that Brad Lawson probably knows him?'

He nodded.

'That Tara's just a nasty piece of work, too, and, before long, Mr Thornton will realise it, so just stick it out until he does.'

When he had gone, Verity sat staring into space. Her mind was working overtime. She had always wondered if she'd find a link somewhere and this seemed to be it. She had a strong feeling that somewhere along the line Paul fitted into this equation, if only she could figure it out. She suddenly remembered she'd arranged to have supper with Felicity that night.

'So, how did you get on when you saw Jake about the new contract?' Felicity asked as she laid the table.

Verity gave her friend a watered-down version of events and Felicity commiserated.

'From next week, I'm being left to manage things at The Garden Trug. It'll take some getting used to, I can tell you. I've really enjoyed my time at March Place.'

Verity refrained from passing on what Liam had told her earlier that evening. Something warned her to be cautious. After all, Felicity still worked with Brad Lawson.

Over supper Verity said casually, 'Has Brad decided if he's going to enter The Italian Water Garden for this award that's coming up?'

'Certainly is, and I naturally assumed you'd be entering yours, too.'

'Fliss, do you happen to have the information about the award handy?'

Felicity looked surprised.

'Surely Brad gave you the details. I came back with a handful of entry forms, after visiting that garden show the other weekend.'

She saw the expression on Verity's face.

'He didn't tell you, did he? Then how

did you find out?'

'Jake mentioned it in passing this evening and I swear that was the first I'd heard of it.'

Felicity jumped up.

'Hang on! I'm pretty certain I've got a couple of spare forms somewhere. How could Brad be so mean as not to tell you? He'd do absolutely anything to promote The Garden Trug and is completely unscrupulous!'

She foraged about under a pile of magazines and pushed a form across to Verity who scanned the details with interest.

'Two contrasting gardens for each entry, and the competitors must have a couple of sponsors, both in the garden business.'

'That's OK, I'll act as one and Bernie can be the other.'

Verity sighed.

'It would have been a challenge, Fliss, but there won't be time to complete another garden now, not if Tara's about to take up the reins shortly, so I'm afraid that counts me out, after all.'

'Verity, if you're that keen then go for it! There'll be a way round it, you'll see, and I promise to keep it quiet that you're entering.'

Verity was suddenly filled with fresh determination.

'All right, I'll certainly consider it.'

Later, over coffee, Felicity said, 'I know I ought to have told you this before, Verity, but with everything that's happened recently, I couldn't bring myself to do so.'

'So go on then, surprise me!'

However, she was completely unprepared for what came next.

'I met Dave Hartley recently, bumped into him at the same garden show where I picked up those forms.'

Verity caught her breath.

'How is he?'

'Fine. He's got his own business now and a steady girlfriend. The thing is, Verity, he's heard on the grapevine that Paul's in Australia and not likely to be returning to England for some considerable time, because he's been arrested on a drugs charge and is awaiting trial.'

Verity swallowed hard.

'I see.'

She had always had her suspicions and now they had been confirmed. Felicity ran her fingers through her hair.

'And you really had no idea of what he was up to? No strange phone calls or odd characters turning up and asking for him at all hours?'

'No, Fliss, I assure you I knew nothing. We weren't living together, as you well know, and he always discouraged me from going to his place, because it was in such a rough area.'

'But you did go a few times, didn't you?' she persisted. 'Didn't you see anything to make you question the sort of company he was keeping?'

She shook her head.

'No. The police questioned me quite extensively, as you're aware, but I couldn't tell them anything. I'm almost certain, however, that in no way was Paul a user and, at the time, I'm not convinced he was a dealer either.'

'Oh, Verity, you're so naïve. How many times did he borrow money off one or the other of us and never pay it back? And then, when the time was right, he made off with our van and several thousand pounds.'

Verity felt nauseous. It still hurt to talk about it, not because of any feelings she still had for Paul, but because she was so ashamed of the way she and her friends had been let down. Felicity was right. She had been naïve. It was true — there had been some very odd types in that house where Paul had lived, but they had always seemed pleasant enough to her, and it had never occurred to her, at that time, that Paul might be involved in something unsavoury. She gave her friend a weak smile.

'Thanks Fliss, you were right to tell me. Let's hope that's an end to it!'

10

The following morning, Verity paid an early visit to Hollybanks. She had worked out a plan of campaign for creating the secret garden, but needed her father's support. He listened intently as she told him what had happened between herself and Jake on the previous day, and about the award scheme.

'Well, of course I'll do whatever I can to support you, Verity.'

After they had finished discussing things, he agreed to advance some money for the necessary items she would require and to loan her Liam for the rest of the week.

Liam was extremely enthusiastic when Verity outlined her ideas for the Garden. At March Place, Mrs Hall informed them that Jake would be away for a few days, making it easier for them to carry out the work involved.

There was now only one corner of the Lady Mary Thornton Garden left to work on, bordering on the area designated for The Secret Garden. As it was obvious there was so little for the two of them to do, they had arranged that, if questioned, Liam would say he had come to do some repairs to the fountain. Within the space of four days, a circular bed was dug out at the end of the garden, the surrounding trees and existing shrubs were cut back and the lawn was laid. It was an easy matter to create a small rock pool, incorporating the underground spring. The Secret Garden was small but charming and, by the end of the week it had taken shape in an amazing way.

The circular bed had been partly filled with rectangular paving stones and coloured gravel, leaving spaces for alpines to grow in between. Liam had showed his skill at woodwork by creating a rustic arbour. Verity chose to plant more summer jasmine and a fragranced climbing rose, to train up it.

On the Friday, Verity was busy deadheading one of the rose bushes in The Lady Mary Thornton Garden when Jake appeared. He looked about him appraisingly.

'Every time I come in here I see something new.'

'I realise we ought to have finished by now,' she said awkwardly. She was standing so close to him that she could smell the fresh woody fragrance of his cologne and her heart began to pound.

She longed to tell him how much she had missed him and that he had hurt her immeasurably by taking Tara's word against hers. Instead, she moved a couple of paces away pretending to examine a plant.

'There's no particular rush,' he said, 'unless you're desperate to get back to Hollybanks. A job worth doing is worth doing well. I must say Brad's made excellent progress on the first stage of the woodland garden.'

So that's what he'd been doing! She

had kept out of his way as much as possible, not wanting any further confrontations.

'It would have been nice if you'd told me about the award scheme,' she said sharply.

It was his turn to frown.

'Oh, come on, Verity, where were you when the discussion took place?'

'No idea, but I certainly wasn't included. Never mind, I've loved working on this garden. Now, if you'll excuse me, I've things to do.'

'Verity!' he implored, catching her by the arm.

'I've got to go. I'm expected at Hollybanks,' she said desperately and, freeing herself, shot off down the path.

She heard him calling her name, but he didn't attempt to follow her. A few more days and she would be back at Hollybanks permanently, so there was no good thinking about what might have been.

A couple of hours in the company of her family that evening soon put things back in perspective for her again. After all, she reasoned, Jake wasn't to know the effect he had on her.

The next morning, she made an early start, and presently Liam joined her. Together they completed the little rock pool and planted the banks with a variety of flowers. Afterwards, they laid some circular stepping stones in the lawn. Liam had found an exquisite little statue with entwined lovers covered in lichen, half buried beneath the undergrowth. They took it to Sam to see if he could clean it up, having discovered he was good at things like that.

Uncle Jack was off home that afternoon, and before he went, he treated the family to lunch at a restaurant in Oakhurst. They would all miss him because he was such a character. Verity realised that there was no longer any reason for her to remain at the lodge but she was reluctant to leave because she loved it there.

She arrived at March Place as usual on Monday, and was putting the finishing touches to the final corner of the Lady Mary Thornton Garden, when Jake turned up, wheeling the statue in a barrow.

'Sam's cleaned this up and I must say I'm rather pleased with the result. Where did you want it?'

'Anywhere will do, thanks,' she said rather unenthusiastically. 'Jake, I'm grateful to you for allowing me to stay in the lodge whilst Uncle Jack's been at Hollybanks, but he's gone home now so I'll vacate it in a day or two.'

'Verity,' he implored, 'it doesn't have to be like this, you know.'

'But I don't know, that's just it. Ever since I've worked here, I've met with opposition from one person or another and now this last episode is the final straw. It's a big disappointment to me that it's had to end in this way.'

He came to stand beside her, so near that she found it unbearable.

'You and I need to have a talk. Now what shall I do with this statue?'

And, before she could prevent him,

he went through the opening in the hedge and into The Secret Garden.

Oh, well, she thought, I might as well be hung for a sheep as a lamb!

She waited and when, after a while, he didn't appear she supposed he had found another way out and went to look. Jake was seated on the rustic bench, staring into the little rock pool. She went to his side, her heart hammering wildly.

'I suppose you're angry that I went ahead without consulting you.'

For a long moment, he did not reply, and then he reached out his hand and, taking it, she sat down beside him.

'Verity, it's beautiful, more beautiful than I could ever have imagined, and this little statue will make it quite perfect! How could I have doubted you for one moment? Forgive me for being so blind that I truly couldn't see what was going on beneath my very nose.'

'I'll try,' she assured him with a half-smile, 'but it won't be easy.'

'I'll have a word with Liam. I want

the pair of you to work here until this garden is finished, if you'd like to, of course.'

'Of course, we would, and it wasn't true, you know. I didn't say any of those things to Tara, even if I might have thought them,' she added honestly.

'There've been too many misunderstandings, things that need sorting out before the garden project can be resumed. Trust me, Verity. It'll be all right, I promise you.'

After lunch, Liam turned up looking pleased as punch.

'Jake Thornton's told me that The Secret Garden's just what he had in mind and wants us to enter for that award.'

They spent that afternoon working in the garden, happy in the knowledge that they had Jake's blessing. Later, as they surveyed their handiwork, Jake came to join them.

'I didn't see how you could improve upon what you'd done already, but that maple is just right. Verity, I've called a meeting so's we can get a few things straightened out. I'm just waiting for the others to arrive now.'

Presently, Verity went along to the dining-room where they were all seated round the large table — Jake, Craig, Brad, Tara and Felicity.

Jake began without preamble.

'Good, now that we're all here let's get started, shall we? Firstly, I'd like to thank you all for the very fine job you've made of the three gardens, each so individual. You've made a sterling effort and I'm delighted with the result. I've called you all together so that you can get a clear picture of what my aims and objectives are for the rest of the garden project. I've done a great deal of thinking over the week-end. I've considered the various proposals put forward by yourselves and now I'm going to outline my own ideas.'

'Would you like me to explain, Jake?' Tara interrupted.

'No, thank you, Tara, this is something I need to do myself. You've all proved you're capable of a commendable standard of work and have brought your individuality to the gardens you've created.'

Brad drummed his fingers impatiently on the arm of his chair. They were all looking expectantly at Jake.

'As I expect you're aware, Verity, Craig and Tara have recently joined forces with The Garden Trug, making it an altogether much bigger enterprise.'

'And Jake's promised to allow me to manage the future development of the gardens here,' Tara said triumphantly.

Jake frowned.

'No, Tara, you didn't listen then and I'm afraid you're not listening now. I'm sorry, but I've got to be fair to everyone. If you think about it, you'll remember that I didn't make any definite promises.'

Craig and Brad were now looking slightly uneasy and Tara had gone red. Verity wondered what Jake was to say next. He leaned back in his chair.

'I've decided that I'm not going to

renew any of your contracts. No, please, let me finish! In future I'm gong to employ individuals, not garden centres, to do my work. As a workforce, you've done a brilliant job, but you don't gel and some of you have been rather ruthless in the way you've gone about things, and so I'm afraid I've got no alternative but to make this decision. There is to be no room for discussion because it's very much a take-it-or-leave-it situation.'

There were gasps from several of those seated round the table. Jake picked up his papers.

'Would those of you who are interested in working for me independently, please remain behind? If you want some time to think things over please feel free to come back to me with your decision tomorrow.'

In answer, Brad got to his feet looking thunderous, followed by Craig.

Tara said in a stifled tone, 'Jake, how could you! You know what this has meant to me.'

'Then you should have stuck to the rules,' he said grimly. 'I don't like dirty dealing and you ought to know that by now.'

Tara shot Verity a look of pure venom.

'I hope you're satisfied now you've got your own way, but you haven't heard the last of this!'

She then stormed out of the room with Jake close behind her, leaving Verity and Felicity still sitting at the table.

'And then there were two,' Felicity said, as the door closed behind them.

'It was all so unexpected. I still can't get my head round it. And you, Fliss, how's all this going to affect you?' Verity asked.

Felicity grinned broadly.

'Couldn't be better. I've decided to sell my shares in The Garden Trug, after all. I don't approve of the amalgamation.'

'So you, for one, would be happy to have a new contract?'

She nodded.

'Certainly would and I know Sean would be pleased, too.'

Jake came into the room just then, followed by Mrs Hall, with a tray of coffee, and a madly barking Prudence, who rushed up to Verity greeting her like a long-lost friend.

As they drank their coffee Jake said, 'Right now, let's get down to business, assuming you're both prepared to continue to work here.'

'Yes, please!' they chorused in unison.

He grinned.

'Good, then hours are to be fairly flexible, like now. Pay and conditions to be negotiable. I shall continue to employ a groundsman to do general maintenance. On top of that, you may recommend a couple of folk to work under your direction, and they will also receive contracts from me. There's a lot to be done so I'll expect you both back here tomorrow and we'll proceed from there and, this time, let's be open with one another. No secrets and no misunderstandings, eh?'

11

The next few days were some of the happiest Verity had experienced in a long while. Liam consented readily to working full-time at March Place, as did Ralph. Bernie was taken on full-time at Hollybanks and his nephew, fresh from college, came to help out as well, so everything worked out fine for all concerned. It was also arranged that Verity should stay on at the lodge until such time as Jake should decide to put it back on the market.

She had just got in on Friday when there was a loud knock. She didn't recognise the man and woman standing outside, and put the chain on the door before opening it a fraction.

'Miss Vernon?'

'Yes,' she said and suddenly felt uneasy.

The man showed her his identity card.

'C.I.D. May we come in?'

They followed her into the sitting-room and she waited expectantly.

'I understand you know a Paul Blackwood,' the male detective said without preamble.

'I haven't seen him for two and a half years,' Verity replied.

The woman smiled at her reassuringly.

'It's all right, Miss Vernon. We're aware of what happened in Sussex.'

Her companion came to the point.

'I believe you also know his half-brother, Bradley Blackwood.'

'No,' she said bemused. 'I'm afraid I can't help you there. I don't know any Bradley Blackwood.'

She stopped. Of course, it all made sense now!

'But I do know a Brad Lawson.'

'That's the one, using an assumed name. We've just had a chat with your friend, Felicity Felton, who works with him. She didn't think you'd made the connection.'

Verity put her hands to her head. Why on earth hadn't Felicity told her that Brad and Paul were related? Something had niggled away at the back of her mind ever since she'd met Brad Lawson on that first occasion. It wasn't that he bore any physical resemblance to Paul at all but her instinct had told her to be wary of him. After a moment she looked up.

'Just tell me what this is all about, please.'

'Drugs,' she was informed. 'Bradley Lawson or Blackwood, as his real name is, has been arrested for being in possession of a large quantity of heroin and we want to know if you can help us with our investigations.'

When they had gone, Verity sat staring blankly into space. She shuddered when she considered the danger she and Felicity had been in. There was so many unanswered questions. For instance, had Brad Lawson followed her here to Oakhurst? Did the others know what had been going on? She had to find Jake.

He was sitting on the terrace and looked up as she approached him. He surveyed her pale face.

'I've been expecting you.'

'How did you know?'

'I was interviewed, too, of course, earlier this afternoon. I had my suspicions, but couldn't prevent Tara from joining forces with Lawson. Just for the record, none of it had anything to do with Craig. He was just going to be used for an innocent cover up.'

'And Tara?'

'Oh, she knew what Brad was involved in all right, but was more interested in using his business to secure a foothold here. Of course, I had no idea Lawson was a dealer when I engaged him to do the work here. Anyway, Tara made the most of his involvement with her brother, who'd been into drugs, to get what she wanted — a partnership in the business.'

'Surely she was playing a dangerous game.'

'Indeed she was, but I think she must have convinced Brad that, with her running the business, things would be greatly improved for him. After all, the garden centre was a pretty good cover for the drug scene, as your friend, Paul, had already discovered. Hopefully, Tara wouldn't have agreed to have anything to do with drugs. Of course, without realising it, I placed her in a great deal of danger by refusing to let her have control of the garden project. Anyway, now she's gone back to her family. Craig is staying put at the Rose Centre and The Garden Trug will, no doubt, be closing permanently, which should be good news for Hollybanks!'

'But who actually grassed on Brad Lawson?'

'It could have been any one of a number of people. Dealers make enemies. I understand the police themselves have had Brad under surveillance for quite some time.'

'I've just learned that Brad was the half-brother of Paul Blackwood, that man that I . . . '

'Yes, it was brought to my attention,' he said gently, wishing he could smooth away all the hurt for her. 'You must try to put it all behind you now.'

'The police believe Brad thought I'd helped Paul get away, because he'd double-crossed him in some drugs-related deal, but, of course, that wasn't true. How naïve I've been. I feel so used.'

He took her hand.

'You weren't to know, so stop blaming yourself.'

'I think both Felicity and Brad must have believed I was still in touch with Paul, although Fliss knows better now. They each had their own reasons for wanting to catch up with him, so that's probably why they chose to come to Oakhurst.'

Jake saw how painful this was for her.

'But, on reflection, why would Brad continue with the gardening business when his brother had already been involved in a similar scam?'

'Apparently the police didn't link Paul with Brad to begin with, because Paul was fostered and they'd both been brought up in different towns. They hadn't had much to do with one another in the past.'

'It's a pity it didn't stay that way,' Jake said grimly.

She nodded.

'Yes, and bags of fertiliser and such must have been a good cover-up for packets of dope.'

Verity stared at him.

'That's it!' she exclaimed. 'Why didn't I realise before? All that vandalism at Hollybanks wasn't mindless at all. Whoever did it must have been looking for something. Our order got mixed up on one occasion with The Garden Trug's. Perhaps some of the illegal substances were delivered to Hollybanks by mistake!'

'It's a possibility, but how do you account for the vandalism here?'

Verity considered this for a moment.

'Perhaps it was to throw the police off the scent and implicate me in some way, rivalry between the garden centres. After all, Brad wasn't exactly keen to have me around, right from the outset, was he?'

Jake spread his hands.

'Nice theory but maybe we ought to leave the police to fathom it all out. Let's have dinner and forget about it for the time being, shall we? I'm famished and very thirsty after all this talking.'

Verity was suddenly aware of her attire.

'But I haven't changed!'

His gaze travelled over her slowly.

'Relax. I'm beginning to get used to the compost! It's part of your image.'

Surprisingly enough, she found she had a good appetite for the tempting food served by Mrs Hall. After trout with almonds, they were enjoying an excellent summer pudding when, quite without meaning to, she found herself saying, 'I thought you and Tara were going to be married, you know.'

He raised his eyebrows.

'Did you now? I suppose I only have myself to blame for any misunderstandings on Tara's part, but she'll get over it, no doubt.'

'Had you known her a long time?' she asked, in spite of herself, as his words slowly registered and she realised that he really had no intention of marrying Tara after all.

'Oh, a few years. Her cousin lives near my family in the Cotswolds. That's how I met her. At one point, she kept rather questionable company, liked wild parties and so her father was pleased when I befriended her, believing I would provide a steadying influence. Unfortunately, she wanted the relationship to be something more permanent and so, when I inherited March Place, she invited herself down here and got into the habit of turning up. You know the rest.'

After coffee, they walked round the grounds. It was such a beautiful summer's evening and the air was filled with sweet fragrances.

'There's such a lot I still don't know about you, Jake, and yet you seem to know everything about me.'

'Not quite everything, just certain things that help me to understand the sort of person you are, talented, sensitive and very caring. So, what is it that you want to know about me, eh?'

'You've never told me how you came to inherit March Place. Sometimes you seem to be, well, remote, as if you're troubled by something.'

A slight shadow crossed his face, as if to confirm what she had just said.

'As I've already told you, my family lives in the Cotswolds.'

'So why don't they visit?' she asked.

'They will, in due course. I wanted to wait until I'd got things in some semblance of order before inviting them. Hopefully, they'll be here for the garden party next month and then you can witness me playing at happy families. As to why I inherited March

Place, my Uncle Thomas knew that nothing would induce the rest of the family to live here and his older brother, who's inherited the title and the bulk of the money from the estate, is perfectly happy to remain where he lives, too.

'I think Uncle Thomas was afraid the old place might be leased out as a country hotel or even sold off, which is why he left it to me. He knew I'd take a genuine interest in restoring it. My grandfather purchased March Place as somewhere convenient to stay when he needed to go to London, but then, when he died, Uncle Thomas and Aunt Mary decided to make it their home. There, does that satisfy you? And, just in case you're wondering, my grandfather left me a substantial sum of money in his will which was held in trust for me until I was twenty-five.'

She coloured, remembering all the speculation. They had reached the Lady Mary Thornton Garden and went to sit beneath a rose arbour.

'But there's something more, isn't there?' she persisted, watching his face. 'Something you're still not telling me.'

'You are being very tiresome tonight! What makes you say that?'

'Intuition. You know about me, and now it's your turn!'

She waited patiently, not taking her eyes from his face, and seeing that there was indeed something else.

'I've put it behind me now,' he told her at last, 'in the same way that you must put Paul Blackwood and all that happened behind you.'

'Then tell me, so that I can stop wondering.'

'When I lived in the Cotswolds, I got married to a very beautiful young woman whom I loved very dearly. We were blissfully happy.'

So that was it! He was already married! She ought to have guessed.

'I'd recently qualified,' he continued, 'and my new job meant I was frequently working away from home. One Friday evening, I thought I'd surprise her, get home early so's we could spent a long weekend together, but when I arrived she wasn't there. She'd gone out that morning with a friend who'd offered her a flight in his helicopter. It crashed and they were both killed. She was four months pregnant at the time and I was utterly devastated. It was as if my whole world had fallen apart.'

'How dreadful,' she whispered, aware of the heartache he must have experienced.

He caught her hand.

'So that's why I've been abroad these past years, but now I've found a haven here in Oakhurst. Come on, it's time we sorted out our own lives.'

'Where are we going?' she asked as he pulled her to her feet.

'I'll give you one guess!'

He led her by the hand into The Secret Garden which that day was truly glorious — an absolute profusion of flowers and perfumes with the musical sound of trickling water coming from the rock pool. He put his arms about her waist and drew her to him. Dark-blue eyes met his slate-green ones questioningly and then he said softly, 'There have been so many misunderstandings between us, and now I think it's high time we spoke about what's truly in our hearts. Verity, what happened to Catherine and my unborn child was something that affected me very deeply at the time, but it was more than eight years ago, and life has to go on. Yes, that was my reason for selling my home in the Cotswolds, and for being such a restless individual. I honestly thought I could never love again, but I was so mistaken!'

Gently he tilted her face towards him.

'I've fallen in love with you, Verity Vernon and, if you could find it in your heart to care for me, my darling, then I'd be the happiest man in the world. Will you marry me, Verity?'

'Oh, Jake, of course I will. I love you as I've never loved anyone before.'

The air was filled with the delicate fragrance of summer jasmine as he kissed her with all the passion that she had yearned for since they had met.

THE END

We do hope that you have enjoyed reading this large print book.

Did you know that all of our titles are available for purchase?

We publish a wide range of high quality large print books including:
Romances, Mysteries, Classics
General Fiction
Non Fiction and Westerns

Special interest titles available in large print are:
The Little Oxford Dictionary
Music Book, Song Book
Hymn Book, Service Book

Also available from us courtesy of Oxford University Press:
Young Readers' Dictionary
(large print edition)
Young Readers' Thesaurus
(large print edition)

For further information or a free brochure, please contact us at:
Ulverscroft Large Print Books Ltd.,
The Green, Bradgate Road, Anstey,
Leicester, LE7 7FU, England.
Tel: (00 44) **0116 236 4325**
Fax: (00 44) **0116 234 0205**

Other titles in the
Linford Romance Library:

THREE TALL TAMARISKS

Christine Briscomb

Joanna Baxter flies from Sydney to run her parents' small farm in the Adelaide Hills while they recover from a road accident. But after crossing swords with Riley Kemp, life is anything but uneventful. Gradually she discovers that Riley's passionate nature and quirky sense of humour are capturing her emotions, but a magical day spent with him on the coast comes to an abrupt end when the elegant Greta intervenes. Did Riley love Greta after all?

SUMMER IN HANOVER SQUARE

Charlotte Grey

The impoverished Margaret Lambart is suddenly flung into all the glitter of the Season in Regency London. Suspected by her godmother's nephew, the influential Marquis St. George, of being merely a common adventuress, she has, nevertheless, a brilliant success, and attracts the attentions of the young Duke of Oxford. However, when the Marquis discovers that Margaret is far from wanting a husband he finds he has to revise his estimate of her true worth.

CONFLICT OF HEARTS

Gillian Kaye

Somerset, at the end of World War I: Daniel Holley, unhappily married to an ailing wife and father of four grown-up children, is attracted to beautiful schoolteacher Harriet Bray, but he knows his love is hopeless. Daniel's only daughter, Amy, who dreams of becoming a milliner and is caught up in her love for young bank clerk John Tottle, looks on as the drama of Daniel and Harriet's fate and happiness gradually unfolds.

THE SOLDIER'S WOMAN

Freda M. Long

When Lieutenant Alain d'Albert was deserted by his girlfriend, a replacement was at hand in the shape of Christina Calvi, whose yearning for respectability through marriage did not quite coincide with her profession as a soldier's woman. Christina's obsessive love for Alain was not returned. The handsome hussar married an heiress and banished the soldier's woman from his life. But Christina was unswerving in the pursuit of her dream and Alain found his resistance weakening . . .